CHANEL JONES

Collision of Grace

J&J
JONES & JONES
— Publishing —

First published by Jones & Jones Publishing 2026

First edition

ISBN: 979-8-9947496-8-5

Editing by Ashely Glover

This book was professionally typeset on Reedsy.
Find out more at reedsy.com

For those who choose obedience when it costs them comfort.
For those who stand when silence would be safer.
For those who trust God not because the road is clear—
but because He is faithful in the dark.

And for anyone who has ever been pulled from the wreckage
and discovered that grace was already there.

Contents

PROLOGUE iii
1 The Red Light 1
2 Pulled From the Fire 4
3 Aftershock 7
4 The Waiting Game 10
5 The Woman in the Rain 14
6 Coffee, Donuts, and Complications 18
7 Fractured 23
8 What Doesn't Line Up 26
9 Statements 31
10 Thresholds 35
11 Release Conditions 39
12 Crossing Home 43
13 First Night, Second Sight 48
14 Present Tense 54
15 Quorum 59
16 Lines We Cross 64
17 The Weight of Quiet 69
18 Patterns 77
19 Pressure Points 81
20 Intentions 86
21 Signals Buried 92
22 Ties That Bind 97
23 By Fire 101
24 Ashes 105
25 False Positives 109

26 Point of No Return 113
27 The Long Night 118
28 Inheritance 122
29 Burn Lines 126
30 The Line Held 132
EPILOGUE 137
Sneak Peek: Grounded by Grace [Book 2] 142
About the Author 146

PROLOGUE

Two Weeks Ago

The Observer

The rain had stopped an hour ago, but the city still wore it.

Streetlights reflected in the pavement like thin, broken ribbons. Water gathered in the seams of the curb, dark and patient, as if it had nowhere else to go. The kind of night that made even expensive buildings look tired—glass towers blinking with scattered lights, security cameras swiveling with quiet certainty, the illusion of order held together by electricity.

The Observer parked two blocks away and walked the rest.

He knew that to an observant onlooker, he might appear paranoid. He didn't care. He was experienced enough to know that being careful often kept you from being killed.

He kept his hands in his coat pockets and his pace unhurried, the way men did when they belonged somewhere. He didn't look over his shoulder. He didn't scan the street with obvious vigilance. He let his attention widen and soften, taking in motion without pinning it down.

A couple argued beneath an awning near a closed restaurant. A taxi idled at the corner, its driver hunched over a phone. A man in a hoodie crossed against the light, head down, moving like someone who didn't want to be remembered.

Normal.

That was always the point.

The building he entered had no name on the street. Just a clean, frosted directory and a keycard reader set into polished steel. The lobby smelled faintly of citrus cleaner and money. A security guard sat behind a desk that looked more decorative than defensive.

The Observer didn't greet him.

He simply lifted his hand—two fingers, a gesture that implied familiarity without inviting conversation—and walked to the elevator bank.

The guard barely acknowledged his presence.

The keycard in the Observer's pocket wasn't his.

But it worked.

The elevator rose without sound. No music. No mirrors. No camera he could see.

He appreciated that. It meant someone understood discretion.

When the doors opened, the corridor beyond was dim and empty, carpet muffling each step. The Observer passed two closed doors before stopping at the third. No plaque. No numbers. Just a narrow seam and a handle too clean to be touched often.

He knocked once, turned the knob, and stepped inside.

Warm air greeted him, carrying the scent of cedar and black coffee.

The office was sparse in the way only powerful men allowed themselves to be. A desk without clutter. Two chairs positioned precisely. A wall of windows that framed the city like a possession. There were no personal photos. No sentimental objects. If there was a life behind this, it was kept elsewhere.

The man stood near the window, back turned, hands clasped behind him. His posture was relaxed, yet still alert. The man embodied the kind of ease that came from believing the world would move when he asked it to. Because it usually did.

He didn't turn right away.

"Traffic?" the man asked.

The Observer stopped just inside the door and closed it behind him with deliberate care.

"No," he said. "Timing."

That earned a quiet exhale—almost a laugh, but restrained.

"Always," the man murmured.

The Observer crossed to the small conference table off to the side. A single overhead lamp lit it like an island. He set down a slim portfolio case and opened it with both hands.

Inside lay a map.

This was nothing like the kind of cheap paper map tourists unfolded at gas stations. This map was printed on matte paper, crisp and heavy, marked with clean lines and tight notations—something never meant to exist outside a controlled environment.

The Observer smoothed it flat.

The man finally turned.

He was older than most men in rooms like this, silver at his temples, his face lined in places that suggested years spent deciding difficult things without apology. His eyes were sharp. And while they were no longer bright with youth, they were not dulled by complacency. They were sharp in the way of people who knew where all the bodies were buried.

He walked to the table and looked down.

The Observer watched his hands as they rested on the map's edge. Strong. Steady. No sign of any tremors.

"This is it," the Observer said.

The man's gaze moved over the printed parcels—small blocks scattered across states, each circled with an efficient red ring. In the margins: dates, routing numbers, entity names that looked harmless in isolation.

Together, they told a different story.

The Observer traced a line with his finger.

"Here," he said. "And here. The corridor holds."

The man nodded once, slow.

"It always held," he said. "It was just... incomplete."

The Observer's jaw tightened.

"Incomplete is a luxury we don't have anymore."

The man's eyes flicked up briefly, measuring tone.

"How tight is the timeline?" he asked.

The Observer didn't look away from the map.

"Thirty days," he said. "Possibly less, depending on scrutiny."

The man made a low sound in acknowledgment.

"Scrutiny from where?"

The Observer tapped a circled parcel near the center.

"From anyone who still believes processes exist for a reason," he said. "A review committee that asks too many questions. A regulator with a conscience. A board member who doesn't know when to enjoy his seat."

The man's mouth curved faintly.

"A board member," he repeated. "Or a CEO."

The Observer's finger paused—just long enough to confirm the thought.

He didn't say the word.

Names were how people got sloppy.

"Once this final acquisition closes," the Observer continued, "the timeline locks. Everything else becomes... automatic."

The man studied the map as if it might confess something.

"And if it doesn't close?"

"Then we lose the window," the Observer said evenly. "We wait. Which means exposure. Variables. Time we don't control."

The man's thumb brushed the edge of the paper.

"You don't like waiting."

"No," the Observer replied. "I like control."

A flicker of amusement crossed the man's face.

"Then we're aligned."

The Observer didn't return the smile.

He slid a second sheet from the portfolio—a list of dates and signatures, an approval chain that looked ordinary at first glance.

Except the names were wrong.

"The purchase is routed through Redfield Holdings," the Observer said. "Option control rather than ownership. This is the cleanest path."

"I approved that structure," the man said.

"You approved the structure," the Observer replied. "But the clock doesn't care about structures. It cares about closure."

He tapped the final circled parcel.

"This is the last gap. If it doesn't close on schedule, the sequence staggers."

The man leaned closer.

"You're certain?"

"Yes," the Observer said. "The pattern completes here. That's why it's been protected."

The man studied him, then nodded once.

"It will get done."

The Observer felt the smallest easing in his chest—and suppressed it.

"How?" he asked.

"I'll apply pressure where it's needed," the man said, smoothing his cuff. "Incentives first."

"And if incentives fail?"

A faint, cold smile.

"Then we adjust."

Adjustments were expensive.

Not in money.

In blood.

The Observer kept his face neutral.

"Once this closes," he said, "the rest won't be gentle."

"Gentle?" the man echoed. "We're not building a charity."

The Observer didn't disagree with him.

"Thirty days," he said, standing.

"You'll have your closure," the man replied, already turning back to the city.

As the Observer reached the door, the man spoke again.

"History doesn't care how clean the beginning is."

The Observer paused.

"It only cares who's left standing at the end."

The door closed behind him.

The corridor felt colder now. The elevator accepted him without question.

In the mirrored seam before the doors shut, he caught his reflection—calm, controlled, forgettable.

Exactly as trained.

Thirty days.

A final parcel.

A system already in motion.

And delay was not an option.

1

The Red Light

Monica Greene was almost home when the sedan blew through the intersection.

One moment, she was cruising toward the green light waiting for her at the edge of town, humming softly to the worship song playing through her speakers. The next—headlights, a violent metallic roar. A silver luxury SUV—large, new, unmistakably high-end—darted around her, moving far too fast for the narrow two-lane stretch as it approached the intersection. Then another set of headlights appeared from the right. The black sedan ran its red light.

"Oh my gosh—"

The impact was deafening. The sedan struck the SUV broadside, spinning it like a toy before it flipped once, twice, and slammed upside down into the ditch beside the road. The black sedan never slowed. Its taillights vanished into the darkness. A hit-and-run.

Monica slammed on her brakes. Gravel skidded beneath her tires as her heart hammered against her ribs. She barely managed to shove the car into park before she jumped out.

"Lord, please," she whispered, already running.

There were no other vehicles on the road. No nearby houses. Only darkness, chirping insects, and the sharp, unmistakable smell of gasoline. She fumbled for her phone and dialed 911 as she slid down into the ditch.

"911, what's your emergency?"

"A hit-and-run," Monica said, breathless. "I'm on County Road 19, near the old mill turnoff. Please hurry. The vehicle's leaking fuel."

"Is the driver conscious?"

"I—I don't know yet." Her boots slipped in the mud as she reached the shattered passenger-side window. "I'm checking now."

Inside, a man hung upside down, held in place by his seat belt. Blood traced a thin line from a cut along his temple, dark against his skin. His breathing was shallow—but present.

"Sir?" she called. "Can you hear me?"

A low groan answered.

Relief surged through her.

"He's alive," she told the dispatcher. "But there's fuel everywhere. I can smell it."

"Ma'am, you need to move away from the vehicle," the dispatcher said firmly. "Emergency units are on the way. Do not approach the car."

A faint flicker caught Monica's eye near the crumpled hood. Her stomach dropped.

"There's a spark", she said, panic tightening her voice. "I can't just stand here."

"Ma'am, listen to me," the dispatcher said, firm and urgent now. "If there's fuel, you are putting yourself in immediate danger. You need to get back—now."

Monica swallowed hard, backing up a step— but her eyes stayed fixed on the man trapped inside.

"I can't wait," she said, her voice tight. "If this car ignites, he won't make it."

There was a pause on the line.

"Okay," the dispatcher said, controlled but tense. "I don't want you touching anything sharp or hot. Stay as far from the engine as you can. Tell me what you're doing."

Monica moved to the passenger side, gripping the edge of the door frame where the metal hadn't buckled completely. She planted her feet, leaned back, and pulled.

Nothing. The metal was folded inward, warped and seemingly immovable. Her breath came fast and shallow. Fear pressed in around her, sharp and disorienting.

"God... please," she whispered. "Help me."

She pulled again. The door groaned—just slightly—but didn't open.

Then she felt it. A subtle shift in the air. Cool. A single drop of rain landed on her arm. Then another. It wasn't a storm, but it was just enough to darken the dust and dull the sharp sting of gasoline in the air.

"Rain," Monica breathed.

"Ma'am," the dispatcher said slowly, "we're not seeing rain reported in your area."

Monica didn't answer. She took a breath, planted her feet, and pulled again—harder this time. The door shrieked as the metal bent. It gave—just enough.

Rain began to fall more steadily now, slicking the dirt beneath her hands, thinning the smoke drifting from the hood.

"Come on," she grunted, gripping the bent frame with everything she had. "Please—move!"

The metal screamed in protest. Then the door finally tore free. Rain drummed against the wreckage, steady and relentless.

Enough.

2

Pulled From the Fire

Monica crawled through the battered passenger-side door, glass crunching beneath her palms. Rain pattered against the underside of the overturned SUV, dripping steadily through cracked seams of metal and plastic.

The man's eyes fluttered open.

For a split second, everything else faded.

They were an impossible, striking blue—clear even through the haze of shock. Dark lashes framed them, incongruous against the blood smeared across his forehead. His jaw was strong, sharply defined, though pain tightened the muscles along it as awareness returned.

"You're... real?" he slurred.

"Yes," Monica said softly. "I'm here. And I'm getting you out."

He blinked, confusion clouding his gaze. "What... happened?"

"You were hit," she said. "The other driver ran."

Something flickered across his expression—anger, instinct, maybe—but it vanished just as quickly.

A tongue of flame licked across the crumpled hood. Rain smothered it almost immediately.

"You're going to need to trust me," Monica said, steadying her voice. "Can you move your arms?"

He lifted one arm an inch before it fell back with a low groan.

"That's okay," she said quickly. "That's enough."

She reached down, fingers searching through the debris until they closed around a jagged shard of glass. Carefully, she shifted her position, mindful of the way he hung suspended upside down.

"I'm going to cut your seatbelt," she said. "When it gives, I've got you. Do you hear me?"

A faint nod.

The dispatcher's voice crackled from the phone wedged between Monica's ear and shoulder.

"Emergency units are four minutes out. Keep him talking. Don't let him lose consciousness."

"Sir," Monica said, sawing at the thick strap, her arms burning, "what's your name?"

He sucked in a breath, pain carving lines across his face. "M... Michael."

"Michael," she repeated, anchoring them both. "I'm Monica. Stay with me."

Thunder cracked overhead, close enough to rattle the metal frame around them. The seat belt finally gave. Michael dropped suddenly into her arms, his weight heavy and unyielding. Monica braced herself, teeth clenched as glass bit into her knees.

"You're okay," she whispered, even as fear flared sharp in her chest. "I've got you."

Smoke curled into the cabin again—thicker now.

"Ma'am," the dispatcher shouted, urgency cutting through the line. "You both need away from the car. Now."

Monica didn't hesitate.

She dragged him inch by inch toward the opening, rain soaking her hair, her clothes, the mud beneath her hands. She hooked her arms beneath his and pulled, muscles screaming in protest.

"Hurts," Michael groaned.

"I know," she said quietly. "I'm sorry. Just hold on. We have to get out of here."

She had him halfway out when the engine popped again—louder this time.

Fear detonated in her chest.

With a cry, Monica hauled him the rest of the way free. A small explosion burst beneath the hood just as they cleared the wreck. Heat flared. Sparks flew.

Rain extinguished them almost instantly.

Monica rolled them both into the wet grass, gasping, heart pounding as she instinctively shielded his body with her own.

"Ma'am!" the dispatcher shouted. "Are you okay? Talk to me!"

A breathless laugh tore from Monica's chest—unsteady, disbelieving.

"We're out," she said, her voice shaking. "We're out."

She looked down at the man beside her. Rain streaked blood across his face, but his chest still rose and fell.

Alive.

Sirens wailed in the distance, faint but growing louder with every second.

Monica pressed a trembling hand into the mud and whispered the only words she had left.

Thank You.

3

Aftershock

Red and blue lights finally cut through the darkness, washing the wet fields in streaks of color. Tires crunched over gravel as patrol cars and an ambulance skidded to a stop along the roadside.

Relief hit Monica so hard her knees nearly buckled.

Paramedics ran toward them, boots slipping in the mud. Monica was still kneeling beside Michael, rain-soaked and trembling, her hands hovering near his shoulders as if afraid to let go.

One of the paramedics dropped to his knees. “Sir, can you hear me?”

Michael groaned faintly.

The paramedic glanced at Monica. “Did you pull him out of the vehicle?”

She nodded, too drained to speak.

He exhaled slowly. “That SUV could’ve gone up. What you did was dangerous. Someone must have been looking out for you tonight but never take a chance like that again.”

Monica swallowed. “I didn’t do it alone.”

They moved with practiced efficiency—securing a neck brace, sliding a board beneath him, lifting Michael onto the stretcher. As they raised him, his hand drifted outward, fingers grasping at empty air.

“Don’t... go,” he murmured.

Before she could stop herself, Monica stepped forward and took his hand.

“I’m right here,” she said softly.

His grip was weak but deliberate, as though he were anchoring himself to the only thing that still made sense.

A paramedic met her eyes, a silent exchange of understanding passing between them. "We've got him now. We'll take good care of him."

Reluctantly, Monica let go.

They loaded Michael into the ambulance. The doors closed with a solid, final clang.

And then—just like that—the rain stopped.

It broke off as if someone had flipped a switch.

The night settled into an eerie stillness as law enforcement took over. An officer approached, notebook in hand.

"Ma'am, I need you to walk me through what you saw," he said gently but firmly. "While it's still fresh."

Monica nodded, though her head felt distant, as if she were underwater.

She told him everything she could remember—how the black sedan ran the light, how it never slowed, the sound of metal tearing, the smell of fuel. She described the sedan as best she could. Black. 4-doors. Going fast. Too fast.

"Anything else?" the officer asked. "License plate? Logos? Damage patterns?"

She shook her head, frustration burning behind her eyes. "It all happened so fast."

"That's okay," he said. "You've done well."

She barely heard him.

Her attention fixed on the ambulance as it pulled back onto the road, siren rising and falling as it disappeared toward town.

Something tugged at her chest—urgent, unrelenting.

Michael had looked lost when they took her hand away.

"I need to go to the hospital," she said suddenly.

The officer glanced up. "Are you hurt?"

She hesitated. "No. But... I pulled the guy out of the car. I need to know that he's okay."

He studied her for a moment, then nodded. "I understand. We have everything you remember, but we may need to follow up later."

Monica didn't hesitate. She jotted down her phone number, signed the statement, and turned to leave.

As she climbed back into her car, mud streaking the floorboards, her hands were unsteady as she put the car into drive. As she pulled onto the road, following the faint glow of the ambulance's lights, a quiet certainty settled deep in her spirit.

This wasn't just an accident.

It was an ordained interruption—a moment God had allowed for a reason she didn't yet understand.

And whatever waited at the hospital, she knew one thing for certain.

She wasn't meant to walk away from it.

4

The Waiting Game

The ambulance doors flew open as they backed into the ER bay, the sudden wash of fluorescent light making Monica squint. Before she could ask whether she was supposed to follow, a paramedic placed a steady hand on her shoulder.

"You saved his life," he said simply. "Come on."

He guided her through the sliding glass doors and straight past triage, waving off questions with the quiet authority of someone who had already decided the truth for everyone in the room.

"This is his fiancée," he called to the nurse at the desk.

Monica stopped short.

His what?

But the nurse didn't even look up. "Name?"

"Monica," she said, swallowing hard. "Monica Greene."

"ID."

The nurse handed her a visitor sticker and scribbled on a clipboard. "Room three. The doctor will update you once he's stabilized."

Fiancée.

Monica opened her mouth to correct it—then closed it just as quickly. If she spoke up, they would send her home. And she didn't know how she knew it, only that she did.

She wasn't meant to leave yet.

Room three was small and overly bright, the hum of machines bleeding through thin walls. Monica sat in a chair that was both too stiff and too soft, her damp hair dripping onto the linoleum as the adrenaline finally ebbed.

Her hands trembled when she looked down at them.

The rain. The metal tearing loose. The way the fire never fully took.

"God," she whispered, barely audible, "what just happened tonight?"

She didn't expect an answer.

What settled over her wasn't confusion or fear.

It was certainty.

Stay.

Time blurred. Doctors moved in and out of the trauma bay. She caught fragments as they passed—

"Head trauma, but stable..."

"Blood pressure's improving..."

"No internal bleeding..."

"Still unconscious..."

Eventually, a nurse with a whose name tag read **Karen** paused beside her.

"You should go home and rest. These nights can be long."

"I'll stay," Monica said quietly.

Nurse Karen hesitated, then offered a small, knowing smile. "Fiancées usually do."

The word twisted in Monica's stomach. But she stayed anyway. By sunrise, the night had settled deep into her bones. Her clothes were still damp. Her eyes burned from exhaustion and tears she didn't remember shedding. She wasn't sure her heart had slowed since the crash.

A different nurse named Bea peeked in. "No change yet, hon. His vitals are strong, though. He's stable."

Stable. Praise God.

The word steadied her—and threatened to undo her all at once.

"I need to run home," Monica said softly. "My dogs—I didn't feed them last night."

Bea nodded. "Go. But come back soon. Sometimes the first person a patient sees when they wake up matters more than we understand."

The words followed Monica all the way home.

Her two rescue mutts, Tucker and Daisy, greeted her like she'd been gone for days. She dropped to her knees as they climbed into her lap, tails wagging furiously.

"Hey, babies," she murmured. "I'm here. I'm okay."

Even as they pressed their warm bodies against her, doubt whispered back. Are you?

She fed them, showered, changed, and moved through her house as if underwater. Everything felt too quiet. Too ordinary. Too wrong.

In the bathroom mirror, she barely recognized herself—curls wild, cheeks blotchy, a faint bruise blooming along her cheekbone.

"You look like you dragged a man out of a burning car," she muttered.

Because she had.

She pressed her palm against the counter and whispered, "Lord... please stay close."

By noon, she was back at the hospital, coffee in hand—one for herself, one she set untouched on the bedside table.

Just in case.

Michael hadn't woken.

She sat.

And stayed.

And stayed some more.

She prayed under her breath. Read Psalms aloud when the room felt too quiet. Adjusted his blanket. Smoothed a stray curl of dark hair from his forehead.

It wasn't because anyone asked her to.

But because something in her spirit wouldn't let her do otherwise.

The room felt sacred.

Still.

Held.

By evening, exhaustion overtook her. She curled into the stiff chair, sweater pulled tight around her, head resting against her arm.

She didn't remember falling asleep.

Only waking to a whisper—rough, uncertain—cutting through the quiet.

"...my angel."

Her eyes flew open.

Michael was awake.

Looking straight at her.

Clear. Conscious.

Alive.

5

The Woman in the Rain

MICHAEL

Michael woke to the low hum of machines and the deep, aching awareness of a body that had taken a brutal hit. But the first thing he noticed wasn't pain. It was peace.

A stillness that made no sense in the aftermath of twisted metal, fire, and fear. It settled over him quietly, without explanation, as if it had been waiting for him to open his eyes.

He blinked up at the ceiling. Sterile lights. Rhythmic beeping. Hospital.

Then he turned his head.

She was there.

Curled in a chair beside his bed, arms tucked into the sleeves of her sweater, she looked like she had simply... stayed. Her skin was a warm, rich brown, luminous even under the harsh lights. Soft curls framed her face, a few escaping their tie and falling forward as she slept.

Long lashes rested against her cheeks, and there was a quiet strength in the set of her features—calm, steady, unguarded.

She was beautiful, yes, but the beauty wasn't what held him. It was the peace that seemed to surround her, even as she slept.

The woman from the ditch. The one who had pulled him from the wreckage. The one whose voice had stayed with him when everything else went dark.

Monica.

Hanging upside down in the car, his half-conscious mind had called her an angel. Now, fully awake, he understood why the word had come so easily. She looked exhausted—almost fragile. And yet he had seen her strength. Had felt it when she pulled him free with nothing but grit and resolve.

He tried to shift, to lift himself just enough to see her better—and instantly regretted it.

Pain tore through his leg and ribs, sharp and unforgiving. A groan slipped out before he could stop it.

Monica stirred at once. Her eyes fluttered open, soft and startled, and she was on her feet in seconds.

"Michael? You're awake."

Her voice did something to him. Steadied him. Warm and grounding, like a hand on his shoulder when the world tilted.

He had thought he imagined her before. But she was real. More real than the machines. More real than the lingering fear at the edges of his mind.

"Hey," he croaked, emotion catching unexpectedly in his throat.

She stepped closer, concern written plainly across her face. "How do you feel?"

"Like I got run over by a truck," he said hoarsely. "Which... I guess isn't far from the truth."

A faint smile touched her lips, but her eyes stayed serious. "I'm so glad you're okay."

Something shifted inside him at that—quiet, unfamiliar.

The doctor arrived. Nurses followed. Questions were asked. Vitals checked. Machines beeped and hummed.

Michael answered when he could, but his attention kept drifting back to her. Her calm. Her gentleness. Her quiet strength.

She wasn't hovering. She wasn't fussing. She wasn't looking at him like he was broken. She was simply there.

He realized he hadn't experienced presence like that in a long time—the kind that didn't ask for anything in return.

The thought pressed in on him, uninvited and persistent.

Why did God send her?

It didn't feel random.

Her voice had cut through the chaos at exactly the right moment. The rain had come when it was needed. And somehow, in the middle of it all, a woman who barely knew him had seen him clearly.

A nurse appeared in the doorway, voice low and apologetic. "Visiting hours will be ending shortly."

Michael felt the words land before he understood why his chest tightened.

Monica nodded, though she didn't move right away. She stood beside his bed, shoulders squared, as if bracing herself against something unseen. She looked at him again, seeming to look beyond just his injuries and into his very being. He felt slightly exposed.

"It's late," she said gently. "I should let you rest."

"Yeah," he said, though the word didn't quite match the pull in his chest. "That'd probably be good."

But he didn't want her to go.

She lingered at the foot of the bed. "Before I leave... is there anything you need?"

He shook his head automatically, then stopped. His fingers found the edge of the blanket, worrying the fabric.

"Monica?"

"Yes?"

He met her eyes—steady, warm, far too kind for someone who owed him nothing. "Would you... call me when you get home? Just to let me know you're safe?"

The question left him feeling exposed the moment he said it.

Instead of deflecting, she nodded without hesitation. "Of course," she said. "I'll call the room phone."

Relief loosened something tight in his chest.

The nurse stepped closer. "I'm sorry, ma'am, but we really do need to wrap up."

"Right," Monica said softly.

She turned back to him one last time.

And then she hugged him.

He hadn't expected it. He hadn't been held like that in years—softly, without agenda, without anything asked in return. No transaction, no unspoken reason, just warmth.

Her arms wrapped around him, careful and warm. His breath caught as something unguarded stirred deep in his chest.

The peace returned—different now. Deeper. Familiar in a way he couldn't place.

When she left, the room felt colder. He stared at the door long after it closed. Later, when the phone rang, and he heard her voice—

"I'm home."

He let out a breath he hadn't realized he'd been holding. "Good," he murmured. "I was waiting."

She talked about her dogs, about nothing and everything, and the sound of her voice softened something inside him that had been hard for a long time. She just... cared.

And when she said she was glad to hear his voice, something shifted—subtle but undeniable. He didn't know what God was doing. He wasn't even sure he remembered how to hear Him anymore.

But tonight—

He felt seen. Protected. Drawn into something bigger than himself. Before they hung up, he heard himself say, "I can't wait for morning."

He meant it.

As sleep claimed him, Michael whispered the most heartfelt prayer he'd spoken in years.

"God... whatever this is... don't let me mess it up."

And finally, embraced in the presence of the Lord, Michael slept. Deeply. Safely. Held by a peace he didn't yet understand—but trusted anyway.

6

Coffee, Donuts, and Complications

MONICA

Monica woke before her alarm.

For the first time in days, she didn't resent the early hour. Her body was tired, but her spirit felt quietly expectant. She lay still beneath the covers and whispered a prayer.

"Thank You for letting him wake up. Thank You for whatever You're doing here. Help me walk in this with wisdom. No getting ahead of You. No fantasies. Just obedience and kindness."

Peace settled gently over her.

She fed Tucker and Daisy, then moved into the kitchen. The familiar ritual of grinding beans and brewing coffee steadied her. This wasn't hospital coffee. This was her favorite blend from the small roastery downtown—rich and dark, with a hint of chocolate in the aroma.

She poured it into a stainless-steel thermos and filled a travel mug for herself. On impulse, she warmed a frozen blueberry muffin, wrapped it in a napkin, and tucked it into her bag.

"Strong coffee and sugar," she murmured. "That feels appropriate."

The dogs watched her grab her keys with deep suspicion.

"I'll be back later," she promised, crouching to kiss their heads. "No chewing the couch."

They were unconvinced.

Sunlight stretched across the narrow road as she drove, turning the fields gold. The intersection where the wreck had happened looked painfully ordinary in daylight. She slowed anyway.

"I remember," she whispered.

At the hospital, she balanced the thermos, her coffee, and a bakery box of donuts. It felt excessive—and also exactly right.

As she stepped onto Michael's floor, a man in a white coat spotted her and paused.

"Ms. Greene?"

She turned. "Yes?"

Dr. Patel smiled warmly. "Good morning. I wanted to catch you before you went in."

Her heart lifted and clenched at the same time. "How is he?"

"Healing," Patel said. "Which means he's in more pain today. His leg took the worst of it—a significant femur fracture. He'll be on crutches for quite a while. Weeks, maybe months."

"Oh," Monica breathed. "Poor guy."

Patel nodded. "But he's strong. And I'll tell you something else—every nurse on this floor has commented that he seems calmer when you're around." His gaze softened. "You make a difference for him, Ms. Greene. More than you realize."

Her cheeks warmed. "I'm just trying to be kind."

"Kindness saves people," Patel said quietly. "Go on. I'll let you in early."

At the nurses' station, Karen and Bea looked up in unison.

"Well, if it isn't our resident angel," Karen said, eyeing the coffee. "You didn't have to do this."

Monica set everything down. "After what you all do every day? Yes. I did."

Bea clasped her hands. "Coffee and donuts?! Michael's right—you're a keeper."

Monica laughed. "He said that?"

"Oh, he's been asking for you since six," Bea said.

Before Monica could respond, the air behind her tightened. Heels clicked sharply against the tile.

"Excuse me."

Monica turned.

The woman standing there looked like she belonged in a boardroom—sleek hair pulled into a low chignon, tailored blazer, designer bag, tablet tucked under one arm. Control radiated from her.

"I'm here to see Michael Lawson," she said. "I need his room number."

Karen's smile remained professional. "Visiting hours start in ten minutes."

"I'm not visiting," the woman replied coolly. "I'm here on business."

Monica stepped aside instinctively, suddenly aware of herself in jeans and a sweater, clutching coffee and sugar.

Karen cleared her throat. "We'll notify you when visiting hours begin."

The woman exhaled sharply and waited, her gaze flicking briefly to Monica—assessing, dismissing.

Karen leaned closer. "You can go on back to Michael's room," she murmured with a wink.

The woman's head snapped up. "He's awake?"

"Yes," Karen said pointedly. "And Ms. Greene here pulled him from the wreck before it exploded."

The woman's gaze sharpened. "You were there?"

Monica nodded. "I happened to be driving by."

"I see," the woman said. "Then I suppose he owes you a visit."

The words were polite. The tone was not.

Monica turned down the hall, her heart quickening. Help me be kind, she prayed. And help me see clearly.

Michael was propped up in bed when she entered.

The moment he saw her, his face softened completely.

"You came."

"As promised," she said, lifting the thermos. "Strong coffee. Not from a machine."

He pressed a hand to his chest. "Bless the Lord and my rescuer."

Monica hesitated as she set the thermos down. "Before I forget," she said quietly, "there's a woman at the nurses' station asking for you. She said it was business. Visiting hours open in a few minutes."

Something flickered across Michael's expression—brief, controlled. "Thank you for telling me," he said evenly.

She glanced up at him as she poured his coffee, choosing not to ask what the look had meant. "How'd you sleep?"

"Better after your call," he admitted. "Woke up once and thought I imagined you. Then I saw the empty chair."

Heat warmed her cheeks.

He took a sip and closed his eyes. "That's... ministry."

"Dr. Patel says you're grumpy today."

"I'm in pain," he said plainly. "Everything hurts."

"Then let me help."

He gestured awkwardly toward the robe. "I can't seem to manage this."

She stepped closer, helping him settle into it, careful of every wire and bruise. When she finished tying it, he was already looking at her.

"Thank you," he said.

"For the robe?"

"For everything."

Without thinking, he opened his arm. She stepped into the hug.

It was deeper than the night before—steady, quiet, unguarded.

"I needed that," he whispered.

"I know."

A knock interrupted them.

The woman from the nurses' station stepped inside.

"Michael," she said crisply. "We have a situation."

His posture shifted—steel beneath the softness.

"Naomi," he said. "Why are you here?"

"The board is deadlocked," she replied. "They won't move without their CEO."

Monica froze.

CEO?

Michael rubbed his face. "This is not ideal timing."

"It rarely is," Naomi said. "That's the downside of being the CEO."

The room felt smaller.

"I can step out," Monica said quietly.

"No," Michael said firmly. "Stay."

Naomi's eyes flicked toward her, irritation barely concealed. Monica remained where she was.

Naomi studied her—measuring, assessing. Michael noticed.

"She's staying," he said calmly.

The words landed heavier than they should have.

Monica felt it then—the subtle shift, like a door closing somewhere she couldn't see. The room no longer belonged only to recovery and whispered prayers. Decisions lived here.

Consequences too.

Monica folded her hands together, steadying herself. She had said yes to staying.

And whatever this was—

it had already begun to move.

7

Fractured

MICHAEL

Michael knew Naomi hadn't come to check on him. She never did anything without an agenda. And he was pretty sure she didn't have a kind bone in her body.

Standing near the foot of the bed, tablet in hand, posture immaculate, she looked like she belonged here—confident, composed, untouched by IV lines or heart monitors.

Michael did not.

Pain radiated through his leg in slow, relentless waves. He hated being horizontal when decisions were being pressed into him. Hated the way vulnerability invited urgency.

"Let's not drag this out," Naomi said. "The board is waiting."

Michael leaned back against the pillows. "I told them I wouldn't sign anything from a hospital bed."

"This isn't just anything," she replied smoothly. "It's a formality. A signature to ratify what's already been approved."

She handed him the tablet. A simple land acquisition. At least, that was how it was labeled.

Michael's jaw tightened. "That land doesn't exist."

Naomi blinked once. Slowly. "What are you talking about?"

"I drove out there," he said. "There's nothing where the coordinates point. No access road. No utilities. No development markers. Just scrub and fencing that doesn't match the survey."

Her expression shifted slightly. "You went out there yourself?"

"I wanted to see it."

A beat passed.

"Of course it exists," Naomi said. "It's been vetted. Surveyed. Approved. You're reading too much into minor discrepancies."

"They're not minor," Michael replied evenly. "They're foundational."

Naomi exhaled—restrained, practiced. "Michael, we've already invested time and capital into this project. Pulling back now creates problems."

"For who?" he asked.

Her gaze sharpened. "For everyone."

Michael shifted slightly, wincing. "I was returning from that site when the crash happened."

Naomi's eyes flicked up, quick as a blade.

"*And*?" she said.

"And someone ran a red light hard enough to flip my SUV," he continued, holding her gaze. "That coincidence bothers me."

Naomi's mouth curved into something that wasn't quite a smile. "You were in an accident, Michael. Trauma has a way of... rearranging perspective."

"Maybe," he said. "Or maybe someone didn't like me doing my due diligence and visiting the site."

She glanced toward the window, where Monica stood quietly, hands folded, watching the traffic below.

"She doesn't need to be part of this conversation," Naomi said.

"She's staying," Michael replied.

Again.

Naomi's expression cooled by a fraction. "You're stalling."

"I'm investigating."

"The board won't appreciate the delay."

"They don't have to."

Silence stretched—a standoff disguised as patience.

Naomi straightened. "Rest. We'll revisit this when you're thinking more clearly."

She turned toward the door, heels precise against the tile. At the threshold, she paused and glanced back.

"Be careful," she said instead. "Prolonged absence creates instability."

Then she left.

The room felt different after that. Michael exhaled slowly and looked at Monica. "I'm sorry you had to hear all of that."

"That's okay."

"Do you think I'm imagining things?"

She met his eyes, steady. "No."

He nodded once. "That deal is wrong. And someone wanted it done badly enough to push."

Monica considered that. "Then maybe the accident *wasn't* random."

The words settled between them—quiet, dangerous.

Outside the window, traffic moved as if nothing had changed.

Michael knew better.

Pressure didn't create fault lines.

It revealed them.

And something had just begun to fracture.

8

What Doesn't Line Up

MONICA

Monica had learned long ago that trouble rarely announced itself. It slipped in quietly—disguised as urgency, buried in fine print, dressed up as "already approved."

Naomi hadn't raised her voice. She hadn't threatened. She seemed to be in no rush.

That, more than anything, unsettled Monica.

"We just need alignment," Naomi said, her tone smooth, professional. "Michael, once you sign, things can move forward without disruption."

Disruption.

The word lingered.

Monica had built an entire career around that word—preventing it, managing it, cleaning up after it. And she knew one thing for certain: real projects didn't fear scrutiny. Only fragile ones did.

Michael shifted slightly in the bed, jaw tight. "I've already said I'm not signing anything today."

Naomi's gaze flicked briefly to Monica, then back. "I understand you're recovering. But the longer this sits, the more unstable it becomes."

Unstable.

Another word that didn't sit right.

"Instability comes from weak foundations," Michael said evenly. "Never from healthy caution."

Naomi's lips curved into something that resembled a smile. "We'll talk again soon."

She turned toward the door, heels precise, posture unchanged.

"Keep the tablet. Review the deal again when you're feeling clearer," she said. "I trust you'll come to the right conclusion."

Then she left.

The door closed softly behind her.

For a moment, the room was quiet.

Too quiet.

Michael exhaled. "She hates being told no."

Monica didn't answer immediately. She sat in the bedside chair, eyes drifting to the tablet now resting between them on Michael's bed.

Naomi hadn't forgotten it.

She'd left it deliberately.

"Can I ask you something?" Monica said, finally.

Michael turned toward her. "Anything."

"What's the land for?" she asked.

He frowned slightly. "What do you mean?"

"What's its function?" she clarified. "Logistics. Operations. Purpose. What does it support?"

Michael hesitated. "It's part of a larger development strategy. Long-term expansion."

"Expansion of what?"

Silence.

Monica tilted her head, studying him.

"Can I ask you something?"

Michael nodded.

"What does your company actually *do*?"

He blinked, caught off guard. "You mean—"

"I mean beyond the pitch decks," she said gently. "Because land is almost never the end goal. Unless you're a farmer."

She leaned back against the chair, thinking aloud.

"Usually there's a chain. You acquire land so you can build infrastructure. Infrastructure supports systems. Systems support operations. And operations serve whatever someone's really after."

Her gaze returned to his.

"So what was the larger development strategy the board sold you on?"

Michael hesitated, then exhaled slowly, remembering language he'd used a hundred times without ever really sitting with it.

"We were pitched regional development," he said. "Long-term infrastructure investment. Strategic land acquisition to support future growth."

Monica listened intently.

"Transportation corridors. Utility access. Data relay points," he continued. "The board framed it as modernization—making underserved regions viable again. Jobs. Stability. Resilience."

He stopped.

The quiet stretched long enough to feel.

"But land wasn't the product," he said quietly. "It was the leverage."

Monica's eyes sharpened. "Leverage for what?"

Michael shook his head once, like he was shaking something loose.

"They said flexibility," he went on. "Optionality. Control over access points before competitors realized they mattered."

He let out a breath. "I told myself it was smart. Forward-thinking."

She gestured lightly toward the tablet. "To me, this kind of feels like a link without a chain."

Michael studied her, curiosity overtaking fatigue. "That's exactly what started bothering me. And for some reason, there was additional urgency tacked on with this deal."

He nudged the tablet toward her. "She wants me to sign it the moment I stop thinking straight."

Monica accepted it carefully, like something volatile. She didn't dive into numbers or legal language. She didn't need to. She scanned for flow. Inputs.

Outputs. Dependencies.

Her brow furrowed.

"This reads like a solution in search of a problem," she said quietly.

Michael let out a slow breath. "Exactly."

Monica looked up. "Has anyone pushed back on it besides you?"

"No," he said. "They keep telling me I'm overthinking it."

She nodded once.

"That's usually what people say when you won't stop asking the right questions."

A faint smile tugged at his mouth. "I've heard that before."

"So have I," she replied. "I used to run community development for the city—until I learned how often *expediency* was just another word for compromise."

His expression shifted, something like recognition passing between them.

"Different companies. Different stakes," she continued. "Same patterns."

She handed the tablet back. "When something doesn't line up operationally, it's either incompetence... or intention."

The word settled heavily between them.

The hospital phone mounted on the wall rang, sharp and sudden.

They both startled.

Michael glanced toward it. "That'll be the board liaison or Naomi's assistant," he said grimly. "They've been calling that line since my phone was destroyed."

Monica waited as he picked up.

"Yes," he said after a beat. "No, I'm not signing today."

A pause.

"I said no."

He hung up and closed his eyes briefly.

Monica leaned back, pulse steady but alert.

This wasn't chaos.

It was control.

"Michael," she said carefully, "may I give you some unsolicited professional advice?"

He met her gaze. "Please."

"Don't confront anyone else yet," she said. "Not the board and certainly not Naomi. At least not until you understand where the pressure is really coming from."

"And how do you propose I do that?" he asked.

"You watch," she said. "You listen. You notice what doesn't make sense—and who needs it not to."

Michael nodded slowly.

Outside, a gurney rolled past. Someone laughed down the hall.

The world carried on.

But Monica felt it clearly now—the shift she'd sensed since the rain.

She wasn't here by chance.

She was here because God had wired her to see what others overlooked.

She closed her eyes briefly and prayed.

Clarity. Wisdom. Discernment.

Whatever came next, she wanted to see it clearly.

When she opened them, Michael was watching her.

"What?" she asked.

"I was just thinking," he said. "If you hadn't been on that road..."

She shook her head gently. "I don't think that's the right question."

He waited.

"I think the question is," she said, voice calm but certain, "who realized you'd seen something you weren't supposed to."

The answer didn't come.

But the silence that followed felt intentional.

And that, more than anything, told Monica they were standing on unstable ground.

9

Statements

MICHAEL

The knock came softer this time—absent Naomi's razor precision. No urgency. Just protocol.

Michael lifted his head as the door opened and two uniformed officers stepped inside—measured, unhurried, carrying the calm weight of routine.

"Mr. Lawson?" the older one asked.

"Yes."

"I'm Officer Ramirez," he said. "This is Officer Collins. County traffic enforcement." His gaze shifted briefly—to Monica—then sharpened with recognition. "Ms. Greene."

She nodded. "Officer."

Ramirez's mouth curved slightly as his brow furrowed in curiosity. "You were the one on scene."

"Yes," she said simply.

He gave a short nod, something between acknowledgment and respect, then gestured toward the bed. "We're here to take Mr. Lawson's statement regarding the accident."

Michael nodded once. "Of course."

Monica moved instinctively to the chair near the window, giving space without leaving. Michael noticed—and appreciated it.

Ramirez pulled out a small notepad. "First, how are you feeling?"

"Like I won't be running any marathons soon," Michael said dryly.

A flicker of a smile crossed Ramirez's face. "We'll keep it short."

The questions were straightforward: time, location, direction of travel, speed.

Michael answered carefully, sticking to facts. He described the green light, the sudden impact, the way his SUV had spun before the world fractured into sound and force.

"Did you see the other vehicle before the collision?" Collins asked.

"No," Michael said. "Just headlights. Then nothing."

"Witness reports confirm a black sedan fled the scene," Ramirez said. "We're canvassing nearby businesses for traffic footage."

Michael nodded. "I assumed as much."

Ramirez glanced up. "Anything unusual leading up to the accident? Road conditions, visibility issues, mechanical problems?"

Michael paused—just long enough to choose restraint.

"No," he said evenly. "Everything seemed normal."

Ramirez made a note, then looked toward Monica. "Ms. Greene—you were the one who rendered aid."

"Yes," she said.

"I appreciate you giving a preliminary statement at the scene," he continued.

Monica inclined her head slightly. "I answered what I could."

Ramirez's expression softened, just a fraction. "You did more than answer questions. EMS noted significant fuel leakage when they arrived."

Michael didn't look at her, but his chest tightened.

"We may need a formal follow-up statement from you later," Ramirez said. "But for now, that'll be sufficient."

"Of course," Monica replied.

Collins cleared his throat. "Do you remember losing consciousness, Mr. Lawson?"

"Briefly," Michael said. "I came to while I was still in the vehicle."

"And the extraction?" Collins asked.

"She got me out," Michael said, without hesitation. "Before the fire spread."

Ramirez closed the notebook. "You're fortunate," he said quietly. "Both of you."

The officers wrapped up within minutes—their presence efficient, respectful, and contained.

"We'll be in touch," Ramirez said as he stood. "And for what it's worth—hit-and-runs like this don't usually stay unsolved."

Michael held his gaze. "I hope you're right."

Ramirez nodded once. "So do we."

After they left, a comfortable silence descended over the room.

Monica returned to the chair beside his bed. "You did well."

"I didn't lie," Michael said.

"No," she agreed. "You didn't."

"But I didn't tell them everything either."

She met his eyes. "Not yet."

He exhaled slowly. "I need more than instinct before I put something like that on record."

"That's wise," she said. "Once you say it out loud, it changes the investigation."

He nodded.

Another knock sounded.

This one was more familiar.

Dr. Patel stepped inside, chart tucked under his arm.

"Well," he said lightly, "you've officially survived police questioning. That's usually the harder part."

Michael huffed a quiet laugh. "I'll take your word for it."

Patel's expression softened as he grew more serious. "I wanted to talk to you about next steps."

Michael tensed. "Okay."

"Your vitals are stable. Neurologically, you're doing well. No internal bleeding. That leg fracture is significant, but clean." He paused. "Assuming no complications, we're looking at discharge in three to four days."

Michael blinked. "That soon?"

"You won't be walking unassisted," Patel said. "You'll need crutches, follow-up imaging, physical therapy—and someone at home with you. But hospitals are for stabilization, not long-term recovery."

Monica felt her chest tighten.

"Someone at home," Michael repeated.

"Yes," Patel said, meeting his gaze. "You shouldn't be alone initially. Pain management, mobility, fall risk—it's not optional."

Patel glanced briefly at Monica, then back at Michael. "We'll discuss arrangements tomorrow."

After he left, silence settled again.

Different this time.

Heavier.

Michael stared at the ceiling. "I live alone."

Monica didn't answer right away.

The thought rested between them—not yet a problem, but a reality waiting to be addressed.

Outside, afternoon light spilled across the floor, indifferent.

The world kept moving.

But Michael knew something had shifted.

The crash was under investigation. The deal had stalled. The questions were multiplying.

And soon—very soon—he wouldn't be protected by hospital walls.

10

Thresholds

UNKNOWN

Michael Lawson had chosen his neighborhood well. Money did that. It built distance. Bought silence. Created the illusion of safety.

The house reflected the choice—modern lines softened by stone and glass, restraint over excess. Wealth expressed through confidence rather than display.

Michael Lawson was smart.

The woman parked and stepped out.

She took in the property with a single measured glance and kept moving.

That was interesting.

Having learned about her humble upbringing, he would have expected her to pause and stare.

She moved with purpose, keys already in hand, shoulders squared as if she belonged there—even though she didn't.

The observer noted her carefully.

Calm. Alert. Aware.

She unlocked the door and disappeared inside.

***

MONICA

The gate slid open smoothly, responding to the code Michael had given her. Cameras tracked her car as it moved through the neighborhood—quiet, manicured, insulated from the world beyond its borders.

She parked in the circular driveway and took in the house as she approached the front door, entering with the key and alarm code he'd provided.

Inside, the house rested in a heavy, watchful silence. The rooms felt undisturbed, the air untouched by movement for hours. Soft gray light slipped through the windows and settled across the furniture, revealing nothing out of place—yet the quiet carried a weight that made every step feel louder than it should have.

Monica paused just past the entryway, the door clicking shut behind her. The air smelled faintly of cedar and something clean, understated. No clutter. No noise. Just space.

Everything had its place.

Nothing invited you to linger.

It felt less like a home and more like a place someone passed through between long days.

This wasn't the house of a man who drifted through life. Every detail spoke of structure—clean lines, neutral tones, art chosen carefully rather than sentimentally. Floor-to-ceiling windows overlooked a backyard that felt more like a private park than a lawn.

Michael lived well. It was evident that every piece of furniture had clearly been chosen with care. Each detail deliberate rather than decorative.

She set her bag down and reminded herself why she was here.

Clothes. Laptop. Medications. Anything he'd need once he was discharged.

The quiet pressed in as she moved from room to room, gathering items with care, resisting the pull to linger over personal details.

A framed photo in the hallway caught her attention.

Michael stood beside an older man—same jawline, same eyes—both smiling in a way that felt earned rather than posed. No caption. No explanation. Just presence.

She nodded once, as if acknowledging something unspoken, and moved on.

In the bedroom, she opened a drawer and stopped.

Inside lay a neat stack of documents—maps, printouts, survey diagrams.

Land coordinates.

She didn't touch them.

Instead, she closed the drawer gently and stepped back.

None of my business.

She gathered the last of the essentials and zipped her bag.

As she turned toward the door, a prickling sensation brushed the back of her neck.

The feeling of being watched.

She stopped. Listened.

Nothing—just the quiet hum of the house settling, the distant sound of wind moving through trees.

Still, her pulse had quickened.

"Lord," she whispered, barely audible, "keep me aware."

She locked the door behind her and walked back toward her car, posture relaxed even as her senses stayed sharp.

* * *

UNKNOWN

She came out sooner than expected.

Carrying a bag.

No hesitation. No distractions.

The observer watched her pause briefly near the driver's door, scanning the quiet street with a sense of awareness civilians rarely displayed.

This one was smart. Smarter than most.

She drove away without incident.

The gate slid closed, sealing the house back into its curated silence.

The observer lingered a moment longer, eyes fixed on the darkened windows.

Michael Lawson was supposed to be dead.

Or, at the very least, incapacitated long enough to remove him from the equation.

Instead, he was awake. Asking questions.

And now there was the woman.

Composed and deliberate, with a presence that refused to be overlooked. She complicated things.

The engine turned over softly, the vehicle pulling away unnoticed.

Adjustments would need to be made.

* * *

MONICA

As Monica stopped at the light, waiting to merge back onto the main road, her phone buzzed.

A message lit the screen.

It's Michael. I logged into the tablet Naomi left. Everything okay?

Monica blinked.

Of course, he already figured it out.

She smiled faintly and typed back.

All good. I've got what you need.

A beat.

Thank you for doing this.

She didn't respond right away.

Instead, she whispered a prayer she hadn't planned.

"God, if this is where You're leading... help me walk it wisely."

The road stretched ahead, calm and unassuming.

But Monica knew better now.

Thresholds weren't just doors.

They were moments.

And once crossed—

There was no going back.

11

Release Conditions

MICHAEL

The hospital never truly rested. It only softened—machines humming lower, footsteps slower, voices kept deliberately quiet. Michael lay awake long after the pain medication dulled the sharpest edges of his leg, staring at the ceiling as the weight of the night pressed in.

Dr. Patel's words echoed anyway.

You shouldn't be alone.

Michael exhaled slowly.

Of *course*, he shouldn't be alone. He couldn't stand without help. Wasn't sure he could shower without assistance. Couldn't move through his own home without risking another fall.

He hated it.

Needing people had never been part of the plan.

For years, he'd built a life that required no one—efficient, contained, predictable. Independence wasn't just a preference; it was currency. Control meant safety.

Now here he was. A shattered leg. A hospital bed. Decisions narrowing around him.

The chair by the window sat empty now.

Monica had left hours earlier—after insisting on stopping by his house to collect a change of clothes, toiletries, and the laptop he'd asked for out of habit more than necessity. She'd promised to return in the morning. He'd nodded, grateful and unsettled all at once.

The room felt larger without her.

"God," he murmured under his breath, voice barely more than air. "I don't know how to do this."

The injury, he could handle. The dependence was another issue altogether.

A weighty silence gathered around him, steady and patient. The kind that makes room for truth.

And then the memory surfaced—uninvited but unmistakable.

Rain. Fire. A calm voice cutting through panic. Hands pulling him free when he couldn't save himself.

You sent her, he realized.

That unexpected truth washed over him.

The frustration didn't disappear, but something beneath it steadied—quiet, immovable.

Michael lay there until the monitors changed shifts and the hallway lights dimmed further, until exhaustion finally pulled him under.

Morning came gently.

Sunlight filtered through the blinds in pale strips, warming the edge of the bed, the IV stand, the empty chair.

A soft knock sounded at the door.

Monica stepped in a moment later, a paper cup of coffee in one hand and his laptop bag in the other. She looked rested enough to function, tired enough to be human.

"Good morning," she said softly.

Michael exhaled, something in his chest loosening. "You came back."

"Of course I did."

She set the bag down and took the chair by the window, exactly where she'd been before.

When Dr. Patel arrived mid-morning, chart in hand, his expression was measured but encouraging.

"You're looking at discharge within the next twenty-four hours," he said. "Pain management is stable. No neurological concerns. Physical therapy will follow up outpatient."

Michael nodded. "And the logistics."

Patel met his gaze. "You'll need someone with you. At least for the first week."

Michael glanced toward Monica before he could stop himself.

She noticed—but didn't comment.

"I live alone," he said.

"I know," Patel replied. "Which limits the options. Either a temporary in-home aide, or someone you trust staying with you."

A stranger.

In his house.

In his space.

Watching him struggle.

Michael's jaw tightened.

After the doctor left, silence filled the room.

Michael broke it first. "I don't have anyone I can ask," he said quietly. "And I won't."

Monica set her coffee down and closed her laptop decisively.

"You don't have to ask," she said.

He turned toward her, startled. "Monica—"

"You can stay with me," she continued, calm and certain. "At least until you're steady. I have a guest room. No stairs. And I work from home."

The words landed heavier than he expected.

"I can't ask—" he started. "You've already done more than—"

"I know," she said gently. "That's why I'm offering."

He stared at her.

"No obligation. No pressure," she added. "But I won't let you believe your only option is a stranger when it doesn't have to be."

Michael swallowed.

"Why?" he asked.

She didn't rush the answer.

"Because God doesn't rescue people halfway," she said. "And because I think this is part of what He's doing—for both of us."

The room felt suspended.

Michael looked away, blinking hard.

"I asked God for strength," he said after a moment. "I didn't expect this version of it."

A faint smile touched her mouth. "Most of us don't."

Silence settled again—but this time it held.

Finally, he nodded once.

"If you're willing," he said quietly, "I'll accept."

Relief crossed her face—brief, unguarded.

"Good."

The hospital phone rang.

Michael let it ring.

In that moment, something broke open. The path forward didn't feel forced.

It felt given.

And beneath the frustration and uncertainty, the truth settled with quiet clarity:

Monica hadn't just happened to be there that night.

She'd been sent.

12

Crossing Home

Discharge paperwork the next morning took longer than Monica expected. Clipboards passed from hand to hand. Instructions were repeated. Medications explained twice. Warnings delivered gently but firmly—the way nurses spoke when they knew a patient would test boundaries the moment no one was watching.

Michael sat propped in the wheelchair, jaw set, patience thinning by the minute.

"Six weeks, minimum," Nurse Karen said, crouching so she was eye level with him. "No driving. No stairs without assistance. And if you think you're 'fine,' you're not."

"Yes, ma'am," he said dryly.

Bea grinned. "We're writing that down as an official diagnosis. 'CEO Syndrome.'"

Monica laughed softly, grateful for the levity. The last few days had wrapped the floor staff into something like family. They'd watched Michael fight pain. Watched Monica return day after day. Watched something quiet and steady take root.

Karen squeezed Monica's arm. "You know where to find us if he gives you trouble."

"Oh, I fully expect he will," Monica said.

Michael shot her a look. "Betrayal already?"

She smiled sweetly. "I'm just being honest."

When the automatic doors slid open and sunlight spilled into the lobby, something shifted in Monica's chest. Leaving felt heavier than arriving had. Hospitals had a way of suspending life—pain, fear, decisions deferred. A fact she knew better than most.

Outside, the afternoon sun felt almost too bright after days of fluorescent light.

Michael pushed himself upright with a quiet grunt, bracing on his crutches as he turned toward Monica's car. For a moment, he wobbled, and Monica stepped in instinctively, one hand hovering near his elbow.

When he straightened fully, she blinked.

He was tall.

Even hunched slightly, leaning on the crutches, he stood several inches above her five-foot-nine frame. In the hospital bed—wrapped in blankets and wires—she hadn't noticed it. Upright, his broad shoulders and long lines caught her off guard.

"You okay?" he asked, noticing her pause.

She smiled lightly. "Yeah. I just forgot how tall you are."

A corner of his mouth lifted. "Occupational hazard."

She helped him into the passenger seat, her mind quietly recalibrating.

As she slid behind the wheel, nerves fluttered unexpectedly in her stomach.

You're just driving him home, she told herself.

Except it wasn't his home.

And that mattered.

They pulled away from the hospital lot, the traffic light, and ordinary. Monica focused on steady breathing, hands firm on the steering wheel.

"Thank you," Michael said quietly after a moment. "For all of this."

She glanced at him. "You don't need to keep thanking me."

"I know," he said. "But I want to."

She nodded, eyes forward.

They merged onto the main road. A dark sedan slipped in behind them.

At first, Monica didn't register it as anything more than a coincidence. Same turn. Same light.

Then another.

She checked her mirrors casually. Then again.

Still there.

Probably nothing, she told herself.

Still, her pulse ticked up.

After a few miles, the sedan dropped back as traffic thickened. Monica exhaled, tension easing just enough to notice.

You're tired, she thought. That's all.

Michael stared out the window, lost in thought. He hadn't noticed.

Good.

She didn't mention it.

When they turned onto the quieter roads leading toward her neighborhood, something else surfaced—self-consciousness.

She hadn't said much about where she lived.

Michael's house had been all glass and stone and quiet authority. Hers was different.

Smaller. Warmer. Older.

Personal.

She pulled into the driveway and cut the engine.

"Well," she said lightly, unbuckling her seatbelt. "Here we are."

Michael took in the house—the wraparound porch, the worn steps, the potted plants shifted for sunlight rather than symmetry. Barking echoed faintly from inside.

"This is nice," he said.

She blinked. "It is?"

"Yes," he said simply. "It looks welcoming."

That wasn't what she'd expected.

She retrieved the wheelchair and helped him inside, moving carefully. Tucker and Daisy skidded into the entryway, tails wagging furiously until Monica gave a quiet command and ushered them back.

"Gentle," she warned. "He's fragile."

Michael huffed. "I heard that."

"Do you feel up to sitting outside for a bit?" she asked. "The patio's flat.

No steps."

"I'd like that," he said.

She guided him through the doors and into a cushioned chair overlooking her garden. Late-afternoon light filtered through the trees, glinting off a stone fountain nestled among flowering shrubs. The sound of water was steady, unhurried.

Michael exhaled. The tight set of his shoulders gave way.

"This," he said quietly, "is not what I expected."

Monica smiled faintly. "Neither was any of this."

She settled into the rocking chair nearby, grounding herself in the familiar sway. The dogs sprawled at her feet, content.

Michael closed his eyes, listening to the fountain, the birds, the soft hum of a world that wasn't asking anything of him.

"God," he murmured, more to the moment than to her, "I don't know how to slow down. I don't know how to let people help me."

His fingers tightened briefly on the armrest.

"But I'm tired of fighting everything alone."

Monica didn't look up. She didn't need to.

When he opened his eyes again, he watched her—steady, present, unhurried. She wasn't trying to solve him or steer the moment.

She was simply there.

Something settled in his chest.

It wasn't clarity or certainty.

But it was rest.

And for now, that was enough.

* * *

The dark sedan idled beneath the shade of a sycamore tree.

The engine was off. The windows were tinted. From the outside, it almost looked abandoned.

It wasn't.

The man in the driver's seat lowered his binoculars as Monica's car turned into the driveway. He reached for his phone—ignoring the one clipped to the dash, but opting for the smaller one tucked into the console.

One button. No contacts.

The line connected immediately.

"He's been discharged," the man said. His voice was calm, practiced. "Earlier than expected."

A pause.

"He didn't go home," he added. "He's with the woman."

Another pause. Longer this time.

"Yes," the man continued. "Same woman from the accident. She brought him back to her place."

He watched the house. The lights came on one by one.

"He's mobile," he said. "Limited, but not out of play."

Silence crackled on the other end.

Finally, the voice returned—low, displeased.

"That complicates things."

"Yes," the man agreed. "It does."

He glanced at the notebook on the passenger seat, names and timestamps written in a careful hand.

"What are your instructions?"

A beat.

Then: "Stand by. We'll adjust."

The man ended the call and slid the phone away.

Across the street, the house looked peaceful. Ordinary. Safe.

He watched it anyway.

Because problems didn't disappear when they survived.

They multiplied.

13

First Night, Second Sight

Dinner came together quietly.

Monica moved around the kitchen with practiced ease, chopping vegetables, stirring a pot on the stove, the soft clink of utensils filling the spaces between conversation. She hadn't planned anything elaborate—roasted chicken, sauteed vegetables, garlic mashed potatoes. Comfort food. Familiar food.

Michael sat at the kitchen table, leg stretched out carefully, crutches propped nearby. Tucker had claimed the space beneath his chair, chin resting on Michael's good foot, while Daisy lay pressed against his calf like a sentry.

"They've adopted you," Monica said, amused.

"I feel honored," Michael replied. "Also slightly trapped."

Daisy's tail thumped in agreement.

The smell of food wrapped around him, warm and grounding. He hadn't realized how long it had been since he'd eaten something that didn't come in disposable packaging or arrive lukewarm after a meeting ran long.

When Monica set the plate in front of him, he paused.

"Thank you," he said quietly.

She glanced up. "You've said that already."

"I know." He picked up his fork. "Still true."

The first bite stopped him.

He closed his eyes before he could help it.

Monica noticed. "That bad?"

"That *good*," he corrected. "I don't remember the last time I ate something that tasted like... care."

The word landed heavier than he'd intended.

She softened, then waved it off gently, refusing to let the moment tip too far. "Well, good. Because you're stuck with it for a bit."

The dogs seemed pleased by that.

They ate without rushing. Talked about small things—her clients, his failed attempts at cooking in college, Tucker's inexplicable fear of the vacuum. The house settled around them as dusk gave way to night, garden lights flickering on outside.

Later, Monica showed him to the guest room.

It was simple but warm—clean linens, a quilt folded neatly at the foot of the bed, a lamp already turned on.

"I'll be right down the hall," she said. "Bathroom's across from you. Call if you need anything."

"I will," he said. Then, more quietly, "Thank you for trusting me with your space."

She met his eyes. "You're not a burden, Michael."

Something in his chest loosened at that.

The dogs followed him in and made no attempt to leave.

"I see how this is," he murmured as Tucker curled up beside the bed.

Monica laughed softly from the doorway. "Good night."

Michael woke early.

Too early.

The house was still, dawn just beginning to stretch pale light across the ceiling. He lay there for a moment, listening—the birds outside, the distant hum of the fountain, the warm weight of the dogs pressed against him.

Peace.

Then the other part of him stirred.

The part that noticed patterns.

The part that didn't rest easily.

The part that asked why.

Carefully, he eased himself out of bed and made his way to the kitchen, wincing as he moved. He set the coffee maker going quietly, ignoring the voice in his head that sounded suspiciously like Monica telling him to sit down.

By the time she appeared—hair pulled back, laptop tucked under her arm—the smell of fresh coffee had already filled the room.

She stopped short.

"Michael."

He winced. "I can explain."

"You're supposed to be resting."

"I am," he said. "Just... upright."

She crossed her arms. "You're impossible."

"Still grateful," he added, handing her a mug.

She sighed, then took it. "Fine. But you're sitting."

"Yes, ma'am."

His laptop sat open on the table.

She noticed immediately.

"Oh no," she said. "What have you been up to?"

"Digging," he replied calmly.

She arched a brow. "Already?"

"Especially now."

They sat in companionable silence for a few minutes, the dogs shifting under the table like they were guarding something important.

Michael's laptop chimed.

He frowned and checked the screen.

Then his expression changed.

"What is it?" Monica asked.

He turned the laptop toward her.

An email. Short. No pleasantries.

Subject: Heads up

Mike—

Emergency board meeting scheduled.

Vote in 48 hours.

Naomi's pushing continuity language.
She's framing it as temporary.
Didn't feel right not telling you.
—Jonah

Monica read it once.

Then again.

"They're not waiting for you to recover," she said.

"No," Michael replied. "They're not."

He leaned back slightly, wincing, eyes fixed somewhere past the table.

"She wants authority reassigned," he continued. "Interim CEO. Emergency powers. All clean. All technically legal."

Monica set her mug down slowly.

"And the deal?"

"If I'm not in the chair," he said, "I don't need to sign it."

The words landed between them.

Heavily.

Monica nodded once. "So the accident didn't even need to kill you."

Michael looked at her.

"It just needed to remove you from the equation," she finished.

The air grew heavy with what was implied.

Then Michael let out a breath that sounded like something collapsing inward.

"I was driving back from that land because something felt off," he said. "I kept telling myself I was being paranoid. That Naomi wouldn't push something she couldn't defend."

"And now?" Monica asked.

"Now I wonder if she didn't expect me to come back at all."

Monica's chest tightened. She had the stark realization that the feeling welling up inside her wasn't panic, but recognition.

"Okay," she said, her tone shifting. "Let's slow this down."

Michael looked at her sharply. "We don't have time."

"That's what they're counting on," she replied. "Urgency is how bad decisions get disguised as necessary ones."

She reached for her notebook—old-school, spiral-bound—and flipped it open.

"Forty-eight hours," she continued. "That tells us two things."

Michael waited.

"One: whatever this deal enables, it has a strict deadline. Something external. Money. Access. Transfer. And two—"

She looked up.

"They believe you're isolated."

Michael almost laughed. "I kind of am."

She didn't smile.

"You're not," she said simply.

The dogs shifted under the table. The fountain outside murmured steadily, unconcerned.

Michael studied her for a long moment.

"You're very calm," he said.

"I'm focused," she replied. "There's a difference."

She slid the notebook toward him.

"If they remove you, they'll move fast, which means mistakes. People get sloppy when they think the threat is neutralized."

"And I'm the threat," he said.

"Yes. But you're also the variable," she corrected. "And so am I."

He considered that.

"Why?" he asked quietly. "Why you?"

Monica hesitated—then answered honestly.

"Because this is what I do," she said. "I walk into broken systems and find where the pressure's coming from. And because God put me on that road."

Her voice softened.

"I don't think He saved you just to keep you alive. We're missing something. And whatever it is, someone's counting on it staying buried."

Outside, the afternoon light shifted, shadows lengthening across the garden.

Forty-eight hours.

Enough time to act.

Far too little to hesitate.

Michael closed the laptop and rested his hands flat on the table.

"Then we don't react," he said. "We prepare."

Monica nodded.

And somewhere, quietly, the pieces finally clicked into place.

14

Present Tense

MONICA

The next forty-eight hours passed quietly.

Almost too quietly.

Michael and Monica fell into something that resembled a routine. He worked from the kitchen table, legal pads stacked neatly beside his laptop, revisiting past deals—timelines, approvals, signatures that now carried more weight than they once had. Monica wrapped up client work from the living room, headset on, voice steady, as if she weren't also tracking the countdown to a board meeting designed to vote a man out of his own life.

They didn't talk about what came next.

They just lived.

There was something unexpectedly intimate about the quiet companionship of it. The shared coffee refills. The hum of two laptops. The brush of his shoulder as he passed behind her in the narrow hallway. She had never lived with a man before—never woken to the low cadence of someone else moving through the kitchen, never ended a day with another presence in the room that wasn't leaving when the clock struck ten.

It wasn't dramatic. It wasn't romantic in the obvious ways. It was steady.

Warm. Uncomplicated.

And dangerously easy to want.

It would have been simple to pretend this was normal. To let the rhythm convince her it could last. To let laughter slip in without calculating its cost. To forget that this was an intermission, not real life.

For her, at least.

Michael didn't seem to allow himself that luxury.

She saw it in the way he refused to linger. The way he caught himself before settling too deeply into the couch. The way he redirected conversations that drifted too close to tomorrow.

From hoping.

The morning of the vote, Monica was pouring coffee when he spoke.

"I'm going."

No preamble. No hesitation.

She froze.

Her first instinct—absolutely not—rose fast and sharp, but she swallowed it. Turned slowly. Studied his face instead.

Determined. Calm. Resolved.

"I'm not surprised," she said.

"You're not thrilled."

"Of course I'm not thrilled," she replied, arching a brow. "You're barely mobile. Michael—"

"I know," he said. "But I have to be there."

She exhaled. "You could observe remotely."

"They're voting on my removal," he said evenly. "I need to see who's comfortable doing it while I'm in the room."

That landed.

Monica leaned back slightly, recalibrating. She didn't like how exposed he would be. How visible. How vulnerable.

She set her mug down. "Then I'm taking you."

His jaw tightened. "Monica—"

"That's not a suggestion," she said. "You don't walk into that room alone. Not today."

He held her gaze, then nodded once. “Okay.”

She stood in front of the mirror longer than usual and told herself it wasn’t vanity. She had to be intentional.

She chose structure over softness—tailored lines, a clean silhouette, heels that grounded her stance without slowing her stride. Curls pulled back into a low bun. Jewelry minimal.

If she was going to be walking into a room built on power, she had to be sure to look like she belonged there.

Michael was already dressed when she returned.

He looked ready for battle—navy suit, crisp white shirt, black wingtips polished to a quiet shine. His hair was smoothed back, sharpening the angles of his face. That was when it clicked. Monica was finally seeing a glimpse of the man who commanded boardrooms with measured control.

She adjusted his jacket, smoothed the fabric where it pulled. When she reached for his tie, he hesitated.

“I can manage—”

“I know,” she said. “Sit. Please.”

Her fingers worked quickly, tying the knot with practiced ease. She adjusted it once, stepped back, and assessed.

“You look powerful,” she said. “That matters today.”

He studied her. This wasn’t the Monica he was used to seeing—the easy curls falling around her shoulders, the softer fabrics, the quiet warmth she carried into a room without trying. Today, every line of her was deliberate. Armored.

And though he understood the reason for it, he found himself missing the softer version of her. “You look dangerous,” he said.

A thin smile. “Good.”

The drive downtown was quiet.

The city seemed to sharpen as they approached—all glass and steel, money made visible. Monica parked, retrieved the wheelchair, and helped Michael settle into it without ceremony.

Together, they rode the elevator up in silence. Michael’s jaw was tight. Monica’s stomach knotted, but she kept her posture tall. Now was not the time to falter.

Michael reached for her hand.

Then he closed his eyes.

"God," he murmured, low and steady. "We're walking into something I can't control."

The weight of his words settled between them.

"Give me clear eyes. A steady heart," he continued. "And the courage to do what's right when it becomes costly."

His fingers tightened briefly around hers.

"Show us what matters. Order our steps. And when the time comes, give us the strength to stand."

The elevator passed the twenty-fifth floor.

"And if there are things I'm not meant to see yet," he added, quieter now, "give me the wisdom to wait. And the strength to speak when it matters."

Monica stood ramrod straight, watching the numbers on the elevator tick by as Michael's prayer filled the small space.

She stood with him—present, aligned—letting the prayer cover them both.

Thirty-eight.

Thirty-nine.

Michael opened his eyes and met her gaze.

"Thank you," he said—not to God this time.

She nodded once. "Amen."

The elevator chimed.

Forty.

The doors opened.

Heads turned as they moved through the office.

Partly because of her. Mostly because of him.

At the boardroom doors, Naomi's reaction was immediate. Surprise flickered—just once—before control snapped back into place. Jonah didn't bother hiding his response. He leaned back slightly, mouth curving.

Monica wheeled Michael forward.

No rush. No apology.

At the threshold, Michael placed his hand briefly over hers.

"I'll take it from here."

"I'll be right outside," she said.

The doors closed.

Monica took a seat in the hallway, posture straight, eyes alert. The assistants moved with the strained efficiency of people who sensed something was wrong but had already decided it was safer not to ask.

Inside, Michael's voice carried just far enough.

"I assume we can begin."

Silence.

No objections.

No greetings.

No welcome back.

Monica exhaled slowly.

The vote hadn't been cast yet.

But the lines had already been drawn.

Monica knew this much with certainty:

Whatever happened in that room would not stay contained there.

15

Quorum

MICHAEL

The room felt different when the doors closed.

Sound dampened. Air thickened. The hum of the city forty floors below vanished, replaced by the quiet gravity of expectation. This was where decisions were shaped discreetly—then felt loudly by people who would never know how they'd been made.

Michael adjusted his position at the head of the table, ignoring the flare of pain in his leg. He'd learned how to sit without advertising discomfort. Weakness invited momentum, and momentum was exactly what this meeting had been built on.

Naomi stood to his right, tablet already in hand. She hadn't asked if he was ready.

She hadn't needed to.

"Let's begin," she said smoothly. "We have quorum."

Around the table, heads nodded. Screens flickered to life. Legal counsel appeared via video, expression neutral, deliberate. The board secretary cleared her throat.

Michael took it all in.

Jonah sat two seats down on the left. Still. Attentive. Watching Naomi—not Michael. That was new.

Across from him, three directors avoided eye contact altogether. He didn't sense outright hostility. But they seemed resolved—as if they'd already moved on.

Naomi clasped her hands lightly. "As you know, this emergency session was called to address continuity concerns following Michael's accident."

Concerns.

Michael resisted the urge to smile.

"The proposal before us," she continued, "is a temporary reassignment of executive authority. Interim leadership. Limited duration. Fully reversible."

She turned slightly, meeting his gaze at last.

"Michael's recovery remains our priority," she said. "But the company cannot afford paralysis."

There it was.

Michael leaned forward, resting his forearms on the table. The movement drew attention. Good.

"Before we vote," he said evenly, "I'd like to ask a question."

Naomi's expression tightened—just a fraction. "Of course."

He didn't look at her.

He looked at the others.

"How many of you have personally reviewed the full documentation tied to the land acquisition embedded in this proposal?"

Silence held—just long enough to confirm what he already suspected.

A man near the far end shifted in his chair. "That wasn't the scope of this meeting."

"No," Michael agreed. "It wasn't."

He turned his gaze back to Naomi. "Which is interesting, considering the interim authority includes the power to finalize that deal."

Naomi didn't blink. "That authority is standard."

"Is it?" Michael asked calmly. "Because I was returning from inspecting that land myself when I was hit."

This time, the silence stretched.

Jonah's jaw tightened, the look in his eyes sharpening into calculation.

Michael continued, voice steady, precise. "There is no infrastructure at the coordinates provided. No access route. No preliminary work. Nothing that supports the valuation presented."

Naomi stepped in quickly. "Michael, this is not the forum—"

"It absolutely is," he said. "Because if I'm removed today, that deal moves forward without my signature."

A murmur rippled around the table—quiet, contained, but real.

Naomi's tone cooled. "You're implying misconduct."

"I'm implying undue urgency," Michael replied. "And asking why."

He shifted slightly, making no effort to hide the wheelchair, the crutches resting beside him.

As evidence.

"I'm not asking you to side with me," he said. "I'm merely asking you not to rush."

He turned deliberately to Jonah.

"Jonah," he said. "You once asked me what mattered more—speed or accuracy."

Jonah swallowed.

"Accuracy," Jonah said finally.

Naomi's head snapped toward him.

Michael held Jonah's gaze. "Then I'm formally requesting a delay. Forty-five days. Independent review. No authority reassignment. No signatures."

The legal counsel cleared his throat. "A delay would require a procedural vote."

Naomi inhaled slowly. The composure held—but something sharp flickered beneath it. "This is unnecessary."

"Then it shouldn't be threatening," Michael said.

Another pause.

The board secretary glanced around the table. "All those in favor of postponing the vote pending review?"

Hands lifted.

Not all.

But enough.

The secretary counted. Then counted again.

Her eyes widened—just slightly.

"The motion carries," she said. "The board will reconvene in forty-five days."

Naomi remained still.

Too still.

"The interim leadership proposal will be reconsidered at that time," the secretary added.

Michael leaned back carefully, pulse loud in his ears.

He hadn't won.

But he hadn't been removed.

Yet.

Naomi closed her tablet with a soft, deliberate click. "Very well," she said. "Meeting adjourned."

Chairs shifted. Screens went dark. People stood too quickly, conversations carefully muted.

As Jonah passed Michael, he slowed just enough to murmur, "You just made this very complicated."

Michael met his eyes. "It already was."

Jonah didn't respond—but his gaze drifted back toward Naomi, thoughtful now. Measuring.

When the room emptied, Naomi lingered.

"You're making this harder than it needs to be," she said.

Michael didn't look away. "Then we agree on one thing."

Her smile was thin. Controlled. "Be careful, Michael. Recovery makes people sentimental."

"And pressure," he replied evenly, "makes people sloppy."

Her smile vanished.

She turned and walked out.

Michael exhaled slowly.

Beyond the glass, he saw Monica in the hallway—posture straight, eyes sharp, already reading what hadn't been said before he reached her.

The vote had been delayed.

For now.

But as he slowly wheeled himself toward the door, the truth settled heavily in his chest:

They hadn't been trying to remove him.

They'd been trying to move around him.

And now that he'd stayed standing—

They would have to move faster.

16

Lines We Cross

JONAH

Jonah never considered himself a bad man.

But he wasn't exactly a good one either.

Early on, he'd learned what success required—how idealism slowed you down, how clean hands rarely held power. You didn't have to break the law. You just had to understand where it bent. Where it blurred. Where no one looked too closely if the outcome was profitable enough.

That understanding had paid dividends.

He'd been at Vanguard Industries barely two years when Naomi approached him the first time. Casual. Confident. As if she were offering a favor instead of a proposition.

Sign off on this property acquisition, she'd said. Convince a couple of the others to do the same. I'll make it worth your while.

And she had.

Over the next three years, it became a rhythm. A deal here. A rerouted approval there. Always just inside the margins. Always deniable. Michael never noticed—or if he did, he trusted Naomi enough not to question it.

Michael Lawson was a straight-laced CEO. Brilliant. Principled. A little arrogant in the way men got when they believed integrity alone made them untouchable.

Naomi, on the other hand, lived in the gray.

She understood pressure. Timing. Incentive. She understood that systems didn't break—they were nudged.

Jonah had told himself that was fine.

Until this deal.

When Naomi brought him the land acquisition a month ago, something felt off immediately. She shared fewer details than usual. The comps were thin. The justifications vague. And when Jonah pressed—gently, carefully—she deflected.

That alone wasn't unusual.

What was unusual was her demeanor.

Naomi was always tightly wound, but this time there was an edge to it. A sharpness beneath her control, like someone holding a lid on something volatile. She snapped once when he asked about timelines. Apologized too quickly afterward.

Jonah had signed anyway.

Old habits.

But he'd kept watching.

So when he was summoned to a closed-door vote regarding Michael's diminished capacity, Jonah didn't hesitate.

He warned him.

And now Naomi was standing in his office.

She hadn't knocked.

The door closed behind her with deliberate care.

Jonah looked up slowly, taking in the rigid line of her shoulders, the barely restrained fury burning behind her eyes.

That surprised him.

Naomi didn't lose control.

"What was that?" she asked quietly.

Jonah leaned back in his chair. "Good to see you too."

"Don't," she said sharply. "You tipped him off."

"He's still the CEO," Jonah replied. "I figured he deserved to know."

Her laugh was humorless. "Don't insult me."

She crossed the room, stopping just short of his desk. Up close, the tension in her face was unmistakable now—jaw tight, eyes bright with something closer to panic than anger.

"That delay," she said. "That forty-five-day stunt—do you have any idea what you just did?"

"I slowed things down," Jonah said. "Which you told me wasn't a problem."

Her lips pressed thin. "Circumstances have changed."

"Because he showed up?" Jonah asked. "Alive. Awake. Not nearly as incapacitated as everyone expected?"

That landed.

Just slightly.

Enough.

Naomi turned away, pacing once, then back. "Michael is... sensitive right now. Trauma does that."

"Funny," Jonah said. "He didn't sound confused. He sounded focused."

Her eyes snapped to him. "Careful."

Jonah leaned forward. "He mentioned something that stuck with me."

Naomi stilled.

"He said he was returning from that land site when the accident happened."

Silence followed.

Thick. Measured.

"And?" she said.

"And you don't find that interesting?" Jonah pressed. "He inspects the property himself—because something feels off—and hours later he's nearly killed at an intersection?"

Naomi scoffed. "You're chasing ghosts."

"Am I?" Jonah asked. "Because the paperwork is thin. And the urgency around this deal—around removing him—feels disproportionate."

Her gaze hardened. "This is bigger than you."

"Then explain it to me," Jonah said. "Because right now, it looks like you're willing to burn the company down to push one acquisition through."

She stepped closer, lowering her voice. "You're asking questions you don't need answers to."

Jonah held her stare. "I've been useful to you. I think I've earned a little clarity."

A beat passed.

Then Naomi smiled.

It didn't reach her eyes.

"Michael doesn't need to be removed," she said softly. "He just needs to stop being in the way."

Jonah's stomach tightened.

"And if he doesn't?" he asked.

Her gaze slid to the window—to the city below, to the illusion of control they all lived inside.

"Then the board will act," she said. "And so should you."

She turned back to him. "Because if Michael continues down this path... he won't be the only one exposed."

There it was.

It went beyond a threat—it was something colder. A reminder.

Naomi straightened, smoothing her jacket. "Get him on board, Jonah. Or don't stand between him and what comes next."

She reached the door, then paused.

"And if you're wondering," she added coolly, "accidents happen all the time. Especially to men who go looking for things they don't understand. At least Michael has the God he prays to."

Her eyes flicked back to him.

"I imagine a man with hands as dirty as yours is on his own."

Then she was gone.

Jonah sat motionless long after the door clicked shut.

He'd crossed lines before.

But this—

This was something else.

Michael Lawson hadn't just been in the way.

He'd been in danger.

And now, so was Jonah.

For the first time in years, the payoff no longer felt worth the cost—and Jonah wondered if the gray he'd lived in was about to turn very, very dark.

17

The Weight of Quiet

MONICA

The boardroom emptied in stages.

Members left in clusters, voices low, eyes averted. No one lingered. No one congratulated anyone else. The meeting had ended, but the tension hadn't dispersed—it had simply relocated.

Next came Naomi.

She exited the room without a backward glance. Her heels struck the floor with measured precision, her posture flawless, as if Michael's unexpected appearance hadn't unsettled her at all. But Monica saw what others might miss—the way Naomi's jaw stayed tight, the way her fingers flexed once at her side before she stilled them.

Control wasn't peace.

It was restraint.

Michael was the last to emerge.

Still in the wheelchair, shoulders squared, face composed in that CEO way that said nothing and meant everything. Monica stood the moment she saw him, scanning him before she scanned the room behind him.

Michael's hand found hers briefly, steady and deliberate. The touch was light but unmistakable.

We're not alone. Stay sharp.

Monica leaned in slightly. "How'd it go?"

His voice was quiet. "We bought time."

Not relief. Not victory.

Time.

Naomi paused at the edge of the hallway, speaking to a man in a suit Monica didn't recognize from the boardroom—legal, maybe, or something adjacent. Her voice stayed low, controlled. Her posture never wavered.

But when Naomi's eyes slid toward Michael—toward Monica—Monica felt it like a temperature shift. Naomi's gaze didn't just see them.

It cataloged them.

Then Naomi turned away, heels clicking, as if nothing had happened.

Michael's jaw tightened. "I need something from my office."

Monica nodded without question and pivoted the chair as Michael guided her toward the corner suite that bore his name on the frosted glass.

Inside, the space felt untouched. Controlled. As if the last forty-eight hours hadn't tried to dismantle it. Michael moved with intention—retrieving a slim leather folder from his desk, sliding a flash drive into his jacket pocket, unplugging his laptop charger with more care than necessary.

Monica watched the door more than she watched him.

Down the hall, voices carried faintly.

Naomi's tone—cool, precise.

Jonah's lower, measured.

Michael closed the drawer with quiet finality. "Let's get out of here."

Monica didn't argue. She pushed him toward the elevators, matching his urgency in his tone. The hallway felt louder now—keyboards clacking, conversations dropping off mid-sentence, the quiet curiosity of people who knew something was happening but didn't know what.

When they reached the elevator bank, Monica jabbed the button once, then again. The arrow lit. A soft chime.

The doors opened.

Inside was empty. A small mercy.

She rolled Michael in, stepped in after him, and turned to face the hallway as the doors closed. She watched the gap narrow, the polished corporate world slicing away.

Just before the doors sealed, Jonah appeared.

"Michael," he said, voice too controlled.

Monica's grip tightened on the wheelchair handles.

The doors paused, held by Jonah's hand.

His eyes flicked to Monica. He didn't smile. Didn't charm. Whatever he usually was, he wasn't that now.

"I need two minutes," he said.

Michael's gaze hardened. "Make it one."

Jonah stepped inside. The doors slid shut.

The elevator began its descent.

Jonah exhaled through his nose—a restrained sound that wasn't quite a sigh. "You didn't just slow them down."

Michael didn't respond.

"You changed the shape of the problem," Jonah added.

Monica said nothing, but her mind filed the words away.

"We got the delay," Michael said.

Jonah's mouth tightened. "Yeah. Forty-five days."

His eyes flicked briefly to the security camera in the corner, then back. "Naomi didn't expect you to show up."

"I noticed," Michael said.

Jonah nodded once, then lowered his voice anyway. "She's going to push around you now, instead of trying to go through you."

Michael's gaze sharpened. "Meaning?"

Jonah hesitated, choosing his words carefully. "The land deal is the clock. And clocks don't stop just because the CEO has a conscience."

Something cold settled in Monica's stomach.

"You're sure it's urgent?" Michael asked.

Jonah's laugh was short and humorless. "I'm sure it's not normal."

The elevator passed the twentieth floor.

Jonah looked at Monica again, and for a split second something human broke through—regret, maybe. Or fear.

"You're doing the right thing," he said to Michael. But the look he gave Monica said something else entirely.

You've involved her.

Michael didn't look away. "You warned me. That's on you."

Jonah nodded once. "I know."

The elevator chimed at the lobby.

Jonah stepped out quickly, as if he didn't want to be seen lingering with them. But before the doors closed, he paused.

"Michael," he said, not meeting his eyes. "Be careful who you trust with the review."

"I trust facts," Michael replied.

Jonah's gaze lifted—brief, weighted. "Facts don't protect you from people."

The doors closed.

Monica let out a slow breath. Her pulse was steady, but her instincts were loud.

"That was... unexpected," she said.

Michael stared at the closed doors. "He's scared."

"Of Naomi?"

"Maybe. Or of whoever Naomi answers to."

The words sat between them as the elevator descended into the garage.

When the doors opened again, the air was cooler, heavier—concrete and oil and shadow. Monica pushed Michael toward her car, scanning as she moved. Panic wasn't useful. Precision was.

Cars sat in neat rows. Shadows pooled where the lights didn't reach. A handful of people moved with heads down, phones in hand.

Then she felt it.

The hairs at the back of her neck lifted.

Instinct.

The kind that had nothing to do with imagination.

She resisted the urge to look over her shoulder and instead adjusted her grip, quickening her pace as they approached the car.

She helped Michael into the passenger seat. He moved carefully, jaw tightening as pain flared.

Once he was settled, she folded the wheelchair, loaded it into the trunk, and slid behind the wheel, hands clammy.

The engine turned over.

"Take the long way," Michael said.

She glanced at him. "You noticed too."

He nodded once.

They pulled out of the garage.

Within a minute, the sedan appeared.

At first glance, it didn't appear to be the same one from the hospital.

Different color. Different make.

Same feeling.

It stayed two cars back through the first light. Then one. Held steady through the second.

Monica kept her face neutral, hands steady. She didn't speed. Didn't brake-check. Didn't let fear drive.

But she took a turn she didn't need.

The sedan followed.

Another turn.

So did it.

"Don't go to your house," Michael said quietly.

"Agreed."

She turned smoothly into a crowded coffee shop lot instead—busy, public, people everywhere.

The sedan slowed. Hesitated.

Then continued past.

Monica watched it in the rear-view mirror until it disappeared.

Only then did she exhale.

Michael stared out the window.

"Okay," Monica said, keeping her voice even. "We're done pretending."

He met her gaze—ice-blue, steady, exhausted in a way that had nothing to do with his leg. "I didn't want you pulled into this."

Her laugh came out low. Honest. "Michael, I crawled into a wrecked SUV to pull you out. I pulled *myself* into this."

He didn't argue.

She drove again—this time toward a different place. She knew neither of them felt comfortable going to her house yet, or even his.

A small church lot on the edge of town. Empty. Quiet. Visible from the road but tucked behind trees.

She parked and turned off the engine.

For a moment, they just sat with the silence and the reality.

Then Michael pulled out his new phone—overnighted, pristine, too clean for what their lives had become. He stared at it like a weapon.

"You're really going to make a call right now?" Monica asked.

"I'm going to protect right now."

He unlocked it and pulled up a contact.

COL. AARON WHITAKER (RET.)

He hit call.

It rang twice.

"Lawson," a low voice answered.

"Aaron."

A pause. Then, "You're alive."

"Last I checked."

"Don't joke. You should've been dead."

Michael glanced at Monica, then forward. "That's the problem."

Silence.

Then, "Talk."

Michael spoke carefully. He didn't let fear creep into his voice. He stuck to facts. The land coordinates. The missing infrastructure. Naomi's urgency. The emergency vote. The delay. Monica saving his life. The car that had just followed them.

When he finished, there was a long pause.

"You're saying this isn't about continuity," Aaron said.

"It's about access."

"And the accident?"

"I think it was convenient."

"All right."

Aaron's silence carried weight.

"You need someone outside your company," he said. "Someone who can pull threads without announcing it."

"You."

"I'm retired. And if this is what it smells like, you need federal eyes."

Monica's stomach tightened.

"Then who?"

"There's a guy. Trevor Hale. He started in the military's legal corps," Aaron said. "Handled investigations most people have never heard about. After that, the Justice Department recruited him. He doesn't chase headlines—he's a straight shooter."

"Department of Justice?"

"He consults on financial crimes that cross into national security. He won't follow ghosts—but if you bring something real, he'll know what to do."

"I don't have enough yet."

"Then build it. Fast. Because if they tried to remove you legally and failed, the next move won't be legal."

Michael glanced at Monica.

"Do you have somewhere safe you've been staying?" Aaron asked.

"Yes. I've been staying at Monica's."

"Don't stay there tonight. Change routines. Watch for tails."

"I'll text you Hale's secure line. And Mike—"

"What?"

"Don't underestimate Naomi. People like her don't gamble unless someone else has promised to cover the loss."

The call ended.

Michael stared at the phone.

Monica let the weight settle.

"Trevor Hale," she said.

"Doesn't scare easily."

"That's what worries me."

The phone buzzed. A text. A name. A number.

TREVOR HALE — DOJ (secure line). Use only when ready.

"So we're really doing this," Monica said.

"I think we already are," Michael replied. "We just didn't have a name for it."

Outside, the light shifted toward late afternoon. The world moved on.

But Monica felt the difference, sharp as ink on paper.

They weren't just dealing with corruption.

They were dealing with someone who believed they had the right to decide who kept breathing.

She reached across the console and rested her hand briefly over Michael's.

"Before we move," she said, "let's pray."

Michael closed his eyes.

"Lord," Monica said softly, "give us wisdom instead of fear, humility instead of arrogance. Guard our steps and our words. Show us what's true, and keep us from reacting to shadows."

She paused. "And since You sent me into this for a reason... help me carry it well."

"Strength," Michael whispered.

"Amen."

He opened his eyes. The calm there wasn't naïve.

It was anchored somewhere deeper than circumstance.

Monica started the engine.

As they pulled out of the lot, she checked the mirror twice.

The road behind them was clear.

For now.

They weren't just surviving anymore.

They were going on the offensive.

And that would force the enemy to move too.

18

Patterns

MONICA

Michael's house felt different at night.

Cooler. Quieter.

Almost... watchful.

They'd stopped at Monica's place first—quickly, deliberately. Long enough to grab clothes, chargers, and the dogs. Long enough for her to lock the door behind her and accept that whatever normal looked like yesterday, it wasn't waiting inside that house tonight.

The security gate sealed behind them with a low mechanical hum, and Monica felt the shift immediately—the way sound flattened, the way the property absorbed movement instead of echoing it. Lights illuminated the drive in controlled intervals. Cameras tracked without being obvious.

There was no comfort here.

Only containment.

Michael had insisted they come here instead.

"Short term," he'd said. "One night. Better cameras. Fewer blind spots."

She hadn't argued.

The dogs seemed to understand the assignment better than either of them.

Tucker paced the main living space once, nose low, then settled near the back doors as if he'd decided where trouble would come from. Daisy claimed the rug beside Michael's chair, positioning herself squarely between him and the hallway.

"Looks like we've been reassigned," Monica murmured.

Michael glanced down, faintly amused. "I definitely feel... supervised."

Michael set up at the dining table—the same table he'd barely used since buying the house. His laptop came out. Legal pads followed. The sterile quiet softened as purpose filled the room.

Monica took the opposite side, jacket draped over her chair, sleeves rolled. This wasn't a living-room night.

This was a build-the-case night.

They stopped examining deals one by one and began layering them—maps over minutes, approvals over transfers, signatures over time. Patterns surfaced quickly once they stopped looking at intent and started tracing access.

Shell entities repeated.

Board approvals clustered.

Parcels appeared where development made no sense—except in proximity to infrastructure.

The threads of control began to appear.

"Here," Monica said finally, turning her screen. "Redfield Holdings. It never owned the land."

Michael leaned in. "Then why is it everywhere?"

"Because it controls the option," she said. "Not the asset. The access."

He sat back slowly. "Which means they can move without triggering an ownership review."

"And without your signature," she added.

That landed.

Michael stared at the screen, jaw tightening. "Naomi's name isn't anywhere near this."

"No," Monica said. "But the same two board members are."

A pause.

"Jonah used to be one of them," Michael said.

"Used to," Monica echoed.

They worked on.

An hour passed. Then another.

At some point, Monica realized her attention had drifted from the data to Michael. The more she learned about the situation, the more clearly she saw the man standing in the middle of it.

The way he refused to gloss over gaps.

The way pain registered without dictating his pace.

The way integrity showed up as restraint rather than noise.

This was the man Naomi had misjudged.

"You don't know how to cut corners," Monica said quietly.

Michael didn't look up. "I do. I just don't like who I become when I do."

She let that sit.

Later, they shifted to the living room—less formal, more human. Monica brought a blanket. Michael objected. She ignored him and laid it across his lap.

She perched on the edge of the coffee table, notebook open.

"The deadline," she said. "The land option expires in thirty days."

Michael nodded. "Which makes forty-five a problem."

"Exactly. Even if the vote stalls, the deal doesn't."

"So the land isn't the endgame."

"It's more of a doorway."

Silence followed—thick in the space between them.

"A week ago," Michael said, leaning back carefully, "I thought my biggest problem was a hostile board."

"And now?"

"Now I'm trying to figure out who's willing to kill over zoning paperwork."

Without thinking, Monica reached out and rested her hand over his.

"We'll get enough," she said. "For Hale. For someone who can't ignore it."

His fingers curled lightly around hers. "I'm glad you're here."

The words were quiet.

They mattered more than she cared to admit.

They shut everything down just after midnight. Discipline dictated the hour. And exhaustion invites mistakes.

Michael moved slowly toward the master bedroom, leaning harder on the crutches now. The dogs followed like an escort detail.

"You okay?" Monica asked.

"I will be," he said. Then, after a beat, "Thank you. For not treating me like I'm fragile."

"You are fragile," she said honestly. "You're just not weak."

He smiled at that.

As she turned to leave, he said, "Monica?"

"Yes?"

"If this gets worse... I don't want you feeling trapped."

She met his gaze evenly. "I'm not trapped."

She paused. "I'm choosing this."

That mattered.

She slept lightly, attuned to every shift in the unfamiliar house.

And somewhere between the low pulse of the security system and the steady breathing down the hall, Monica understood two things with absolute clarity:

They were closer now—closer than circumstance alone could explain.

And whatever was coming next wouldn't care about that at all.

Which meant they would have to be ready—

Together.

19

Pressure Points

MONICA

The next few days passed without ceremony.

No explosions. No confrontations. No sudden revelations.

Just work.

Michael sat at the dining table with his laptop, legal pads stacked beside him, sleeves rolled back like he was preparing for surgery instead of an investigation. Monica moved between client calls and quiet research, her own laptop open, screens tiled with spreadsheets, filings, and maps that refused to agree with one another.

They worked differently.

Michael traced authority—signatures, approvals, timing.

Monica traced flow—money, purpose, dependency.

Everywhere they looked, something didn't line up.

Land parcels changed hands between shell entities with no operational need. Valuations jumped without justification. Review committees approved acquisitions they never seemed to discuss.

Too clean.

Too fast.

Too quiet.

By the second evening, the dining table looked like a war room.

"This isn't sloppiness," Michael said, rubbing a hand over his jaw. "It's deliberate. Whoever built this expected no one to slow it down."

Monica didn't look up. "They also expected no one to look sideways."

She turned her laptop toward him, highlighting a timeline. "These transfers don't stand alone. They align with infrastructure access points—fiber routes, data corridors. Someone's building leverage."

Michael's eyes sharpened. "You're saying the land itself isn't the goal."

"No," she said quietly. "I think it's the cover."

The room settled into silence—heavy, considering.

Later that night, Michael made the call.

He said only what needed to be said. Using the secure contact Colonel Whitaker had provided, he sent a short message.

This is Michael Lawson. I was told you understand when financial anomalies overlap with national interest. I have documentation. I'd like to meet.

The reply came an hour later.

Day after tomorrow. Noon. I'll send an address. Bring only what you can explain.

Monica read the message over his shoulder.

"That's... encouraging," she said.

Michael exhaled. "It's a start."

The next morning, Michael insisted on going out.

"Just coffee," he said. "I need to see someone."

Monica didn't argue, but she drove.

Jonah's favorite coffee shop sat on a quiet corner downtown—industrial brick, long tables, the kind of place where people pretended not to notice who sat where. The air smelled like espresso and cinnamon, conversations kept low and curated.

Michael spotted Jonah immediately.

Same seat. Same drink. Same careful posture.

"Of course," Michael muttered.

Monica stayed back near the counter, watching from her periphery as Michael crossed the room on his crutches. Jonah looked up, surprise flickering across his face before he masked it.

"Well," Jonah said dryly. "This is unexpected."

"So was the vote," Michael replied. "Mind if I sit?"

Jonah hesitated, then nodded.

They skipped pleasantries.

"I need you to hear this carefully," Michael said. "I'm not asking for your loyalty. I'm asking for the truth."

Jonah's jaw tightened. "You're assuming I have something to give."

"I am," Michael said evenly. "Because you warned me. And because you're still here."

Jonah leaned back slightly. "You think that makes me brave?"

"No," Michael said. "I think it makes you conflicted."

Jonah scowled.

Michael continued, lowering his voice. "This deal—whatever it is—it's bigger than a boardroom play. And Naomi isn't the top of it."

That did it.

Jonah's eyes flicked to the windows, then back. "You shouldn't be saying this out loud."

Michael leaned in just enough to close the distance. "You've been helping her blur approvals for years. I know. I didn't want to know. But this time, you hesitated."

Jonah's throat bobbed. He stared at his coffee.

"You don't know what you're stepping into," he said finally.

"I know enough," Michael replied. "And if you're already in this deep, your silence won't save you."

Jonah's fingers tightened around the cup. "You think I don't see the pressure? The timelines? The urgency?"

"Then help us," Michael said. "Before someone decides you're a liability."

Jonah didn't answer.

Michael waited a beat, then stood carefully. "I'm meeting with someone tomorrow. Federal. You don't have to come with me. But if you have anything—documents, messages, anything at all—don't wait."

Jonah looked up. "And if I do nothing?"

Michael met his gaze. "Then you'll spend the rest of your life hoping this ends without you."

He turned and walked away.

Monica joined him at the door without a word. Through the windshield as they pulled out, she watched Jonah still sitting there, coffee untouched.

He didn't move.

* * *

Naomi arrived unannounced that afternoon.

Jonah barely had time to minimize his screen before she stepped into his office, the door closing behind her with deliberate care.

"You met with Michael Lawson," she said.

Jonah folded his hands. "We ran into each other."

Her gaze sharpened. "In public. In daylight. After a delayed vote."

Jonah leaned back. "He's still the CEO."

"For now," Naomi said coolly. "Which is why optics matter."

Jonah studied her. "Why are you so concerned?"

Naomi's smile was thin. "Because I don't like unpredictability."

She stepped closer. "And I don't like finding out after the fact."

Jonah felt the shift then. Naomi had been careful not to make an outright accusation. But she was assessing him.

Naomi turned toward the window, looking down at the street below. "Be careful, Jonah. People who hesitate tend to draw attention."

Jonah swallowed. "From who?"

Naomi glanced back at him. "From everyone."

She left without another word.

That night, Jonah didn't go home right away.

He took three turns he didn't need. Walked two blocks out of his way. Paused once—just to see what would happen.

The same car stayed with him.

Far enough back to look incidental.

Near enough to feel intentional.

Persistent.

By the time he reached his apartment, his hands were shaking.

Jonah locked the door, leaned against it, and closed his eyes.

He'd crossed lines before.

But now the lines were behind him.

And ahead of him was a choice he could no longer delay.

Tell the truth.

Or keep running until there was nowhere left to go.

Outside, somewhere below, an engine idled.

And Jonah realized—too late—that being useful had finally made him visible.

20

Intentions

MICHAEL

The message came just before dusk.

Tomorrow morning. Same place. I'll bring what I have.

—Jonah

Michael read it twice. Then once more, slower.

No dramatics. No qualifiers. Just enough commitment to matter—and enough ambiguity to be dangerous. He locked his phone and leaned back carefully, letting the weight of the day settle into his bones.

Monica stood at the sink, rinsing dishes, sleeves rolled to her elbows. He was quietly grateful they'd returned to *her* house—her kitchen, where the air smelled faintly of basil and garlic. Simple, grounding things. Things that had nothing to do with boardrooms or shadowed deals.

His own house was immaculate. Luxurious. Designed for control.

This space was warmer. Lived-in. Human.

"Jonah's in," Michael said.

She didn't turn right away. "In enough?"

"He says he'll bring proof."

That earned him a glance—measured, analytical. "Then we assume that makes tomorrow important."

Michael nodded. "That's why I want to take you out."

She blinked. "Out?"

"To dinner," he clarified.

She dried her hands slowly. "Michael—"

"I know," he said gently. "I'm not asking for anything from you. I just... need to say thank you like a man, not a charity case."

Something softened in her expression. Caution didn't vanish—but it stepped aside.

"All right," she said. "Dinner."

* * *

The restaurant was quiet. Intimate without being secluded. Public enough to feel safe. Michael had chosen it deliberately—no white tablecloths, no power-dining energy. Just warm light and real food.

They talked about small things at first. How she'd come to adopt her dogs. Books. A terrible documentary Monica had watched purely out of spite. Michael laughed more than he had in weeks.

At some point, the conversation slowed.

Michael set his fork down.

"I want to be clear," he said. "About us."

Monica stilled—tensing slightly as she shifted her attention to him.

"I don't know what happens next," he continued. "I don't know how long this gets complicated before it gets better. But I do know this—"

He met her eyes.

"You matter to me, Monica. Beyond the crash. Beyond everything that's happened since. My interest in you is real. And when the ground under our feet is steady again, I'd like the chance to pursue this properly."

Her breath caught—just slightly.

"I see you," he said. "I respect you. And I want to build something on truth instead of circumstance."

She studied him for a long moment.

"Thank you for saying that," she said finally. "Honesty matters more to me than grand gestures. And I'd very much like that."

He smiled faintly. "Well, you can count on getting a healthy dose of both."

When dinner ended, they rose from the table together. There was no need to stretch the evening beyond what it had already become. The moment felt complete.

As they slowly walked to the car, Monica slipped her arm lightly through his, careful of his crutches.

The contact was simple. Steady. But it carried weight.

They drove back to her place in comfortable quiet, the kind that didn't need filling. Monica unlocked the front door, the familiar creak of the hinge greeting them as the dogs stirred and padded forward, tails thumping in relief.

Michael paused just inside, taking in the ordinary safety of it—the lamp by the couch, the shoes by the door, the quiet proof of a life rooted and real.

He felt it then.

Recognition.

Two lives that had collided under unlikely circumstances were now choosing to move in the same direction.

He could tell Monica felt it too—the steadiness beneath the uncertainty.

There was no rush in it. No illusion.

Just clarity.

And somewhere deeper than explanation, he felt the quiet, unshakable assurance that God did not bring people together randomly—and that whatever waited ahead of them, they were not meant to face it separately.

***

Morning came quickly.

They arrived at the coffee shop ten minutes before Jonah had promised. Michael chose a table near the window, back to the wall. Old habits resurfaced easily.

Monica sat across from him, notebook open but untouched.

Ten minutes passed.

Then fifteen.

Michael checked his phone.

Nothing.

At twenty minutes, Monica's jaw tightened. "Is it like him to be late?"

"No," Michael said. "It isn't."

At thirty, the barista approached cautiously.

"Michael?"

He looked up. "Yes."

She slid a padded envelope across the counter. "A man dropped this off earlier. Said you'd know what to do with it."

Michael didn't touch it right away.

"Did he say anything else?" Monica asked.

The barista shook her head. "Just that he was sorry."

Michael picked up the envelope.

It was heavier than it should've been.

Inside: a flash drive. Printed emails. Handwritten notes—Jonah's handwriting, tight and slanted. Approval chains. Side agreements. Names that didn't belong on land deals.

Concrete.

Monica exhaled. "He chose."

"Yes," Michael said quietly. "And now he's running."

He sealed the envelope again. "Which means we don't wait."

* * *

The museum was busy without being crowded—school groups, tourists, and researchers scattered through quiet halls. Neutral ground. Public. Watchful without feeling exposed.

Trevor Hale stood near a gallery entrance, hands in his coat pockets, posture relaxed but alert. Early forties. Tall. Clean-cut. The kind of man who didn't scan a room nervously—he absorbed it.

When Michael approached, Trevor's gaze flicked briefly to the crutches.

"Lawson," Trevor said. "You look better than expected."

"Still upright," Michael replied. "For now."

Trevor's mouth curved slightly. "That'll do."

His attention shifted to Monica, precise and unreadable.

"Trevor," Michael said, "this is Monica Greene."

Trevor studied her for a beat, eyes sharp with interest.

"So you're the variable," he said. Then, approving, "A woman to be reckoned with. I like that."

Monica met his gaze without blinking. "I've been called worse."

A quiet huff of laughter escaped him.

Michael shifted subtly closer to her, the movement small but deliberate—an unspoken boundary drawn with calm certainty.

He handed over the envelope.

Trevor tucked it under his arm.

"Walk with me," he said.

They moved through the exhibits at an unhurried pace, footsteps muted by carpet and history. Trevor spoke without looking at either of them.

"If this is what I think it is," he said, "it won't move fast. And it won't move clean."

"We understand," Michael replied.

Trevor stopped near a display of ancient maps—inked borders drawn by men who had never seen the full world they claimed to chart.

"I can't promise outcomes," Trevor said. "Only to process it."

"That's enough," Michael said.

Trevor turned, meeting his gaze fully now. "Once I look at this, you don't get to step back."

Michael didn't hesitate. "We already crossed that line."

Trevor nodded once. "Then let's see who else has."

He opened the envelope at last.

The paper made a soft, unmistakable sound as it slid free—thick, deliberate, final. Trevor scanned the contents in silence, his expression unreadable, attention absolute.

Michael felt the shift.

Fear had passed. Relief hadn't arrived.

What settled instead was momentum.

Whatever came next would not be quiet.

And it would not be contained.

But something fundamental had changed.

They were no longer reacting.

They were choosing their direction.

21

Signals Buried

TREVOR

Trevor didn't bring the file upstairs right away.

He reviewed it again in his office first—door closed, blinds half-drawn, phone powered down. He didn't rush. Rushing was how people missed patterns. Missed intent.

The materials Michael Lawson had handed over were worse than he'd expected.

They were meticulous.

Too meticulous.

Shell corporations layered three deep. Ownership routed through holding companies designed to blur responsibility—entities registered in places known less for transparency than tolerance. Land parcels scattered across multiple states, each one defensible on its own. Agricultural zoning. Light industrial. "Future development."

Benign.

Until Trevor overlaid the maps.

He pulled up a second screen.

Then a third.

Electrical transmission corridors first—the high-voltage lines that fed major population centers along the eastern seaboard. Substations positioned like quiet arteries, regulating the flow of power from generation sites to cities that never slept. Places where a single failure wouldn't just cause an outage, but cascade—forcing manual resets, delayed recovery, and regional instability.

His jaw tightened.

He layered telecommunications next.

Fiber relay stations. Switching hubs. Points where data traffic was consolidated before being routed outward—cell service, emergency communications, financial networks, air traffic coordination. Facilities designed for efficiency, rather than defense.

Then cellular infrastructure.

Towers positioned to blanket metro areas, highway corridors, and ports. Nodes that supported not only calls and data, but also GPS timing, logistics coordination, and emergency response.

Every parcel Michael's company had been pressured to acquire sat near one of those points.

Not directly on top of them.

But close enough.

Close enough to disrupt.

Close enough to control access.

Close enough to delay repairs, block technicians, restrict movement under the cover of ownership rights, and zoning disputes.

This wasn't about real estate.

It was leverage.

Trevor leaned back slowly and exhaled through his nose.

"Okay," he murmured. "Now we're talking."

If someone wanted to cripple the country, they wouldn't start with explosions.

They'd start with dependencies.

Power that didn't fully go out—but couldn't stabilize.

Communications that failed just long enough to confuse.

Systems that corrected themselves... until they couldn't.

The kind of damage that turned modern life brittle.

He compiled a report and took the file to his supervisor an hour later.

Director Susan Calloway listened without interrupting. That alone was unusual.

She flipped through the documents once. Twice. Her expression didn't change—but something behind her eyes did. Calculation. Distance.

"This is circumstantial," she said finally.

Trevor blinked. "It's coordinated."

"It's speculative," Calloway replied. "And it involves corporate actors, not foreign governments."

"Corporate actors don't accidentally buy land next to power substations and data relays," Trevor said evenly. "Not at this scale. Not with this precision."

Calloway closed the folder. "You're reaching."

"I'm connecting," he said.

Silence settled between them.

When she spoke again, her tone had shifted—careful now. Measured.

"There's no current authorization to pursue this as a national security matter," she said. "And no verified intelligence indicating an imminent threat."

Trevor felt the temperature drop.

"Then where did the signals go?" he asked.

Her eyes flicked up—glancing furtively toward the door.

"Excuse me?"

"The indicators," he pressed. "Network mapping. Infrastructure probing. Dry runs disguised as maintenance noise. There's always chatter before something like this. It doesn't just appear."

Calloway stood. "That's enough."

"Someone buried it," Trevor said. "And you know it."

Her voice hardened. "You're crossing lanes."

"No," he replied quietly. "Someone else already did."

She stepped closer, lowering her voice. "Trevor, listen to me. You do not want to pull on threads you don't understand."

His stomach tightened.

Her tone left no room for interpretation.

Back in his office, Trevor didn't sit.

He locked the door and powered up a secure terminal he hadn't touched in months. Old habits came back easily.

He accessed archived logs—reviews closed early. Reports reclassified mid-stream. Anomalies marked as non-actionable that should have triggered escalation.

There it was.

A gap.

Deliberate.

Information redirected just enough to keep oversight fragmented. Power, communications, and finance—each monitored by a different agency, each assuming someone else was watching the whole.

No single picture.

No single owner.

Something cold settled in Trevor's chest.

This wasn't just corruption.

This was premeditation.

* * *

Across the city, in a room without windows, the response unfolded exactly as planned.

An investigator had asked the wrong questions.

The review hadn't stalled—it had surfaced.

The land acquisitions were no longer enough on their own.

Delay was no longer tolerable.

Plans shifted. Fallbacks activated. The timeline narrowed.

One message was sent.

Then another.

Advance schedule.

Remove variables.

* * *

Trevor sat alone as dusk crept across the city.

The map still glowed on his screen—the quiet precision of it, the way the parcels wrapped around the country's spine like fingers testing for weakness.

Michael Lawson hadn't been targeted because he was powerful.

He'd been targeted because he'd noticed.

And Monica Greene—

Trevor closed his eyes briefly.

She was just a civilian. She was never supposed to be part of this.

He reached for his phone and typed a single message.

You need to leave tonight. Both of you. Do not stay where you are.

He hesitated only once before sending it.

Because if he was right—

They weren't dealing with a future threat.

They were already late.

22

Ties That Bind

NAOMI

Naomi knew Jonah was gone before anyone said his name. His office was dark. His calendar was wiped clean. His assistant claimed he'd taken a personal day—but the lie had been rehearsed too carefully. Jonah didn't take personal days. He took exits.

Naomi closed the glass door behind her and stood still, letting the silence settle. The building hummed softly around her—power uninterrupted, systems intact. The illusion of order remained. But something had shifted.

She crossed to her desk and opened the folder she'd already checked twice that morning. The files were still there. So were the approvals. The access logs told a different story. Copied. Downloaded. Exported. Jonah hadn't panicked. He'd prepared.

Naomi felt her pulse quicken, but her expression never wavered. She had learned early—long before boardrooms and leverage—that fear was only useful when kept private.

She reached for her phone.

Jonah could wait. Legal wouldn't help.

Instead, she made the call she'd been avoiding since Michael Lawson wheeled himself back into her life.

The line connected immediately.

"Come up," the voice said. "Now."

Gavin Kincaid's office occupied the top floor alone. He didn't need the space. He preferred distance. Privacy. Solitude.

Naomi stepped out of the private elevator and crossed the quiet expanse without slowing. Floor-to-ceiling windows framed the city like a possession. Gavin stood with his back to her, hands clasped behind him, posture relaxed in a way only men who believed themselves untouchable ever achieved.

"Jonah ran," Naomi said.

Gavin didn't turn. "Of course he did."

"He copied files," she continued. "I don't know how much."

"Enough to be inconvenient," he replied mildly.

Naomi tightened her grip on her tablet. "He could go to Michael."

Gavin smiled faintly. "He already has."

That stopped her.

Gavin turned then—silver at his temples, expression calm, eyes sharp in a way that had nothing to do with age.

"You taught him to hedge," Gavin said. "You taught him to survive. Don't be surprised when he does."

Naomi swallowed. "Then we need to contain this. Quietly."

"Quiet left the room when Michael Lawson didn't die," Gavin said.

The words were casual. Too casual.

Naomi's stomach dropped.

"You said—" she began.

"I said the accident would solve the obstruction," he corrected. "It didn't. Adaptation is required."

She took a step forward. "We've never—"

"Taken decisive action?" Gavin asked. "Naomi, please. Don't pretend innocence now."

Her jaw tightened. "This is different."

"Yes," he agreed. "It is."

He moved past her slowly, deliberately, like a man circling a chessboard.

"Michael isn't corrupt," Gavin continued. "He isn't distracted. And now he's not alone."

Naomi's voice lowered. "That woman. Monica."

Gavin nodded. "A variable you didn't account for."

"I didn't know she'd—"

"You knew enough," he cut in. "And now she knows enough."

The room felt smaller.

Naomi straightened. "We can manage this through the board. Through process."

Gavin stopped in front of her. "Process failed."

His gaze hardened. "So we move to protection."

Naomi's breath caught. "Protection for who?"

"For family," he said simply.

The word landed like a weight.

Naomi's voice wavered, just barely. "You're talking about killing him."

Gavin studied her for a long moment.

"I'm talking about removing risk," he said. "Permanently."

Her pulse roared in her ears. "And her?"

Gavin didn't hesitate. "She's collateral."

Naomi recoiled before she could stop herself. "No."

The word echoed louder than she intended.

Gavin's expression cooled.

"No?" he repeated.

"This isn't what we do," she said. "We influence. We redirect. We don't—"

"We don't get sentimental," he cut in. "You didn't when you stepped into that company. You didn't when you signed off on the first shell. You didn't when you let men like Jonah profit."

She clenched her fists. "That was business."

"This is survival," Gavin said.

He stepped closer, lowering his voice. "Something is coming, Naomi. Bigger than Lawson. Bigger than his conscience. The grid. The systems. The country's illusion of control."

Her breath stuttered. "You're talking about—"

"A reset," he said. "And when it happens, I will not have my daughter exposed because she suddenly remembered her scruples."

The word *daughter* tightened something in her chest she'd spent years keeping buried.

"You are protected," Gavin continued. "You are positioned. You are safe—as long as you stay aligned."

"And if I don't?" she asked quietly.

His smile returned. Cold. Certain.

"Then you'll learn," he said, "what happens to people who mistake proximity to power for immunity."

Silence stretched between them.

Naomi looked at the city beyond the glass. The lights. The order. The lie.

She thought of Michael's eyes in the boardroom. Of Monica's presence—steady, unafraid. Of Jonah's conscience convicting him enough to run.

She nodded once.

The gesture conveyed understanding, rather than allegiance.

"I'll handle my end," she said.

Gavin's gaze softened, satisfied. "Good girl."

The phrase made her skin crawl.

As she turned to leave, her hand trembled—subtle, involuntary. It hadn't done that in years. She stilled it immediately.

And as the elevator doors closed, one truth rang louder than the rest:

They had crossed a line she could not uncross.

And if she didn't decide soon who she answered to—

The choice would be made for her.

23

By Fire

MICHAEL

Michael woke to the sound of dogs barking.

The sound sliced through the house—high, fractured, urgent. Urgent in a way that cut straight through sleep and into instinct. Tucker's bark ricocheted from the back of the house in short, explosive bursts. Daisy's joined in from the hallway, closer, frantic, and protective.

He was upright before pain caught up with him, adrenaline overriding instinct as his foot hit the floor and fire lanced through his leg in protest. He reached for the crutches by memory, heart already racing.

The house was dark. Too dark. No soft glow from the hallway nightlight. No hum of electricity. No ticking clock.

The power was out.

His phone was in his hand instantly. No signal. No bars.

That was when the smell hit him.

Smoke.

Thick enough to taste. Close enough to spike his pulse.

"Monica," he called sharply.

No answer.

The barking had moved toward the back of the house. Urgent. Desperate.

Michael pushed down the hall, breath shallow, every instinct screaming that they were already behind. Smoke thickened as he reached the kitchen, curling along the ceiling in gray fingers.

Then he saw it.

Fire.

Not outside. Inside.

Flames climbed the back wall near the patio doors, racing up the curtains like they'd been invited in. Heat pressed against his skin, dry and punishing.

Accelerant.

This wasn't an accident.

"MONICA!"

She emerged through the smoke, coughing, eyes wide but focused. Her phone was in one hand, her keys in the other.

"Back door's blocked," she said, voice tight. "The hallway too. It's spreading fast."

Michael's mind snapped into motion.

"Front," he said. "Now."

The dogs circled them, frantic, barking and whining. Michael barked commands, forcing calm into a voice he didn't feel. Monica grabbed the leashes, her hands shaking just enough to notice.

The fire roared behind them as they moved—too fast, too loud, too alive. Smoke burned Michael's lungs as he forced himself forward, every step a brutal negotiation between speed and collapse.

The front door was hot when Monica touched it.

She yanked it open.

Air rushed in like mercy.

They burst onto the lawn as the windows behind them shattered inward with a sound like gunfire. Flames surged higher, greedier, devouring the structure as if it had been waiting.

Michael stumbled, crutches slipping on the grass.

Monica caught him.

They went down together.

The dogs broke free, barking wildly.

Behind them, the house groaned—a deep, awful sound—and then the roof began to cave in.

Total loss.

Sirens wailed somewhere in the distance. Too far. Too late.

Michael rolled onto his back, chest heaving, eyes fixed on the inferno that had been Monica's home only hours earlier. The heat drove them farther back, relentless.

"This wasn't a threat," Monica said hoarsely. "This was meant to eliminate us."

Michael nodded, throat too tight to speak.

Headlights cut through the smoke.

A dark SUV skidded to a stop at the curb.

The driver's door flew open.

"Michael! Monica!"

Trevor Hale.

He moved fast—decisive, controlled—already assessing injuries, escape routes, the fire's spread. He hauled Michael up without hesitation, bracing him with practiced efficiency.

"We're not waiting for first responders," Trevor said. "This wasn't random. And it won't be isolated."

Neither Monica nor Michael argued.

Trevor ushered them into the vehicle, dogs scrambling in after them. As he pulled away, the house collapsed fully, flames roaring into the night like something victorious.

Michael watched it disappear in the rear-view mirror.

Everything Monica had built.

Gone.

Trevor drove hard but clean, avoiding main roads, eyes constantly checking the mirrors.

"They moved faster than I expected," Trevor said grimly. "Which means they knew I had the evidence."

Michael closed his eyes.

"So they came for us."

"Yes," Trevor said. "And they won't miss twice."

The SUV slowed as they turned onto a narrow road lined with trees. No streetlights. No neighbors.

A safe house.

Inside, doors locked and the perimeter secured, Trevor finally turned to face them.

"This is no longer about exposure," he said evenly. "It's about survival."

Michael nodded.

Since the rain-soaked night that had started all of this, he'd been circling the truth.

Now it landed.

Full. Heavy. Undeniable.

They hadn't stepped into a storm.

They had uncovered a war.

And the fire had made one thing unmistakably clear—

The stakes had just been raised.

24

Ashes

MONICA

Trevor didn't linger.

He walked them through the safe house with efficient calm—pointing out the locks, the cameras, the emergency exit hidden behind a false panel in the laundry room. He left two phones on the counter, burner-clean and already programmed. Promised to be back in the morning.

"I'm not going far," he said, meeting Monica's eyes in a way that felt deliberate. "Try to get some rest."

Then he was gone.

The door closed behind him with a solid, final click.

And something inside Monica finally gave way.

The silence struck first. A hollow, echoing quiet. The kind that comes after destruction. The safe house was minimal, all neutral tones and borrowed space. Nothing of hers. Nothing familiar.

Her home was gone.

The one she'd worked for. Budgeted for. Built her life inside. The garden she'd tended. The couch where her dogs had slept. The walls that had held laughter and prayer and ordinary, beautiful days.

Gone.

Taken in an instant by people who didn't know her name—and wouldn't care if they did.

Michael turned from the door, sliding the deadbolt into place, checking the lock twice. He moved carefully, favoring his leg, jaw tight with concentration.

"Michael."

The word fractured as it left her mouth.

That was as far as she got.

The weight rushed in all at once—hot and crushing, like smoke filling her lungs. Weeks of swallowed fear. Exhaustion. Anger. Grief. The realization that this hadn't been an accident or a misunderstanding, but a choice made by people willing to erase lives for momentum.

Her knees buckled.

She didn't hit the floor.

Michael was there instantly, arms around her, solid and sure, catching her before she fell. He didn't ask what was wrong. Didn't tell her to breathe. He just held her—anchoring her while the storm broke loose.

She clutched him like the ground itself had vanished.

He guided her to the couch, easing them both down, never breaking contact. She folded into him, forehead pressed to his shoulder, her body shaking with silent sobs she couldn't seem to stop.

"I'm here," he murmured. Low. Steady. "I've got you."

Her tears soaked into his shirt. She didn't apologize. Didn't pull away. She couldn't.

Everything she'd been holding together—professional calm, strategic focus, careful courage—collapsed into raw, unfiltered anguish. Her chest ached like it might split open.

"They burned it," she whispered at last. "Everything. My home. My life."

"I know," he said softly.

"They're so..." Her voice broke. "So heartless. All of this—for greed. For power. They didn't even hesitate."

Michael's hand moved through her hair in slow, grounding strokes. He knew he couldn't fix this for her, but at least he could lend her his presence.

"I'm so sorry," he said quietly. "For pulling you into this."

She shook her head against him. "God put me there," she said, though her voice trembled. "I know He did. But I'm so tired of being afraid."

His hold tightened just slightly.

"So am I," he admitted.

They sat like that for a long time.

Eventually, the sobs slowed. Her breathing evened, though the ache remained—deep and bruised.

Michael's voice was quiet when he finally spoke.

"I don't know how you do it," he said. "Trust God like this. Not just... believe. But trust."

Monica didn't answer right away.

The quiet turned thick as she considered his question.

"It hasn't always been easy," she said finally. "And it wasn't always like this."

He turned slightly toward her. Waited.

"My parents died when I was younger," she continued, eyes fixed somewhere beyond the room. "A car accident. They both ended up on life support. I prayed for them to be healed. I believed God could do it."

She swallowed once.

"He didn't."

Something tightened in Michael's chest.

"But He was there," she said quietly. "Not in the way I begged for. Not even in the way I thought I wanted. But in the middle of it. During. After. When everything hurt, and nothing made sense."

She looked at him then.

"That's when I learned the difference between God fixing things and God staying."

Her voice didn't waver. Because while it still hurt to talk about, it no longer ruled her.

"So when everything falls apart now," she added softly, "I don't assume He's gone. I assume He's close."

Michael didn't respond.

He couldn't.

The questions that had chased him since the accident—the anger, the doubt—fell strangely quiet in the wake of the flames.

He wasn't asking where God had been.

He was wondering if God had been holding him the whole time.

The safe house hummed around them—the faint buzz of the refrigerator, the muted click of the security system cycling. Outside, the world continued, indifferent and intact.

Monica stayed curled into him, letting herself feel the truth she'd been too busy to name.

God had brought her into this.

And He had not abandoned her here.

She rested her cheek against Michael's chest. His heartbeat was steady beneath her ear. Real. Alive.

"I don't know how much more I can carry," she said quietly.

"You don't have to carry it alone," he said without hesitation.

She believed him.

God had placed him here with her. And his presence didn't feel like a coincidence or mere convenience.

It felt like provision.

She closed her eyes.

The fire was still in her lungs. The smoke still clung to her clothes. But beneath the adrenaline and the tremor in her hands, something steadier surfaced.

Surrender.

Lord, I'm still here.

And I trust You to meet me here too.

Michael rested his chin lightly against her hair.

Outside, beyond walls and cameras and locks, forces were still moving. Plans still unfolding.

But for this moment—for this small, sacred pocket of stillness—Monica allowed herself to be held.

And that was enough.

25

False Positives

TREVOR

Trevor should have gone home.

He told himself that twice as he turned into the DOJ parking structure—once when the concrete ramp swallowed his headlights, again when he killed the engine and sat there, listening to it tick as it cooled.

But the file Jonah sent wouldn't let him sleep.

Neither would the way Michael Lawson had looked at him—steady, resolved, already counting the cost. Trevor recognized that look. He'd worn it once himself.

The building was quiet at this hour. Too quiet.

He badged in, nodded to a lone security guard who barely looked up, and took the elevator to his floor. The lights hummed overhead as he walked, his footsteps echoing down the corridor.

He unlocked his office, stepped inside, and closed the door.

The familiar smell of paper and recycled air greeted him. Nothing appeared disturbed. No drawers open. No screens glowing.

Still, something felt off.

Trevor crossed to his desk and woke his terminal. Logged in. Pulled up the internal case folder he'd reviewed earlier that afternoon—the one tied to infrastructure anomalies and flagged grid access points.

The screen blinked.

Then refreshed.

Empty.

Trevor frowned.

He tried again. Different pathway. Archive view.

Nothing.

His pulse ticked higher—dread welling up inside him. He opened system logs, fingers moving faster now, bypassing surface-level access and dropping into backend activity.

That was when he saw it.

Edits timestamped less than an hour ago.

His credentials.

His ID.

Requests logged under his name—data pulls he hadn't made. Queries he hadn't run. Redirections to dead directories. Flags overridden.

A slow chill crept up his spine.

"No," he murmured.

Someone hadn't just erased the evidence.

They'd reassigned ownership of the erasure.

Trevor pulled up access history. Cross-referenced badge swipes. Camera logs.

The same pattern repeated.

His name.

His clearance.

His digital fingerprint.

Clean. Efficient. Surgical.

They weren't burying the trail.

They were redirecting it.

Toward him.

Trevor leaned back in his chair, breath steady, mind racing.

The move was deliberate.

Preparatory.

Someone was setting the stage.

If this surfaced tomorrow—if questions were asked, if oversight committees started sniffing around—they would determine they had a mole.

And that mole would be him.

He closed his eyes briefly.

Lord, give me clarity.

The prayer wasn't dramatic. It didn't need to be. He'd learned long ago that panic dulled judgment, and fear made people sloppy.

And someone here had already made a mistake.

They'd moved too fast.

Trevor logged out of the terminal and stood, scanning the room with fresh eyes. His laptop bag sat where he'd left it. His coat hung on the back of the chair.

He crossed to the window and looked down at the city lights. He'd gotten Michael and Monica to safety—for now. And here he was, standing in a building that had quietly decided he was expendable.

Trevor returned to his desk and pulled a small notebook from the drawer. No markings. No identifiers. He wrote three words on the first page.

Assume compromise everywhere.

Then he shut the notebook and slipped it into his coat.

He didn't take anything else.

No files. No devices. No paper trail.

Whatever he needed now would have to live somewhere that didn't answer to servers or supervisors.

As he reached for the door, his phone buzzed.

A system alert.

Unusual activity detected on your account. Please contact IT Security immediately.

Trevor stared at the message for half a second.

Then he turned the phone off.

He left his office without locking the door.

He wanted it to look like he'd been interrupted.

The elevator ride down felt longer than usual. He kept his posture relaxed, eyes forward, breathing even. When the doors opened in the lobby, the security guard glanced up this time.

"You working late, Hale?" the man asked.

Trevor nodded. "Something like that."

He didn't break stride.

The night air outside felt sharper, colder. Trevor crossed the lot quickly, unlocked his car, and pulled out without turning on the radio.

Only once he was several blocks away did he allow himself to exhale.

They'd erased the trail.

They'd framed the investigator.

Which meant two things were now certain.

First: whatever Michael Lawson had stumbled into was far bigger than a corporate land deal.

And second—

The timeline had just moved up.

Trevor reached for his phone once he was safely on the freeway, powered it back on long enough to send a single encrypted message.

Change of plans.

They're burning records and setting me up.

You're not safe. Neither is Monica.

Don't leave the safe house until I contact you.

I'm going dark. Call only if it's urgent.

He shut the phone off again and drove.

Behind him, the DOJ building glowed calmly against the night sky.

A fortress of glass and steel.

And somewhere inside it, someone was already preparing the narrative of his fall.

Trevor tightened his grip on the wheel.

They wanted a mole.

He only prayed he had enough time to prove they'd chosen the wrong man.

26

Point of No Return

MICHAEL

Michael read the message from Trevor. Then read it a second time.

He didn't move right away.

Monica was still asleep against him, her weight warm and trusting, her breathing uneven—the kind that came only after grief had wrung everything else out of her. One of the dogs lay pressed against the couch, the other stretched at their feet. The room was dim, stitched together by the quiet rhythm of her breath and the steady thud of his heart beneath her cheek.

Carefully, he shifted—slow enough not to wake her—easing her fully onto the cushion. He tucked the blanket back around her shoulders the way she'd done for him more than once. She stirred, murmured something soft and unintelligible, then settled again, her fingers curling briefly where his arm had been.

Guilt tightened his chest.

Pain flared as he stood, sharp and punishing, but it grounded him. Pain meant he was still upright. Still breathing. Still able to choose.

Lord, he prayed silently, give me truth—even if it costs me everything.

He looked at her one last time—curled inward, vulnerable, homeless because of choices he hadn't made but couldn't outrun.

Her home. Gone. Because of him.

Michael grabbed a pen and wrote quickly, leaving the note where she would see it the moment she woke.

I had to step out. I'm safe. I'll explain. I promise. Trust me.

The dogs whined softly as he reached for the door, nails clicking against the floor.

Michael paused, crouching just long enough to scratch behind familiar ears.

"I'll be back," he murmured. "You keep her safe for me."

Then he was gone.

* * *

Naomi's house was lit.

Too lit for after midnight.

The front door opened before Michael rang the bell a second time.

Naomi stood there, robe immaculate, hair perfect, eyes sharp and unreadable.

"You shouldn't be here," she said.

"No," Michael replied evenly. "But neither should I have survived that intersection."

Something flickered across her face—gone as fast as it appeared.

She stepped aside.

The house was quiet in a way that wasn't peaceful. Everything in its place. Nothing personal. Control disguised as comfort.

"I trusted you," Michael said as the door closed behind him. "I defended you. When people questioned your urgency—your methods—I shut them down."

Naomi folded her arms. "You always believed you were protecting me."

"I was," he said. "Until you stopped protecting me back."

Her jaw tightened.

"And now Monica's house is ashes."

Naomi's composure cracked. "That wasn't supposed to happen."

Michael froze.

"Not supposed to happen," he repeated softly.

Confirmation.

"You knew," he said. "You knew I was in the way."

"I didn't order it," Naomi snapped.

"But you didn't stop it."

She looked away.

"I was good to you," Michael said quietly. "I gave you power. Autonomy. Trust."

A voice answered from behind her.

"And that," it said calmly, "was your mistake."

Michael's blood went cold.

Footsteps sounded from the back of the house—unhurried, confident.

A man stepped into the light.

Gavin Kincaid.

Chairman of the Board.

The real one.

"Michael Lawson," Kincaid said pleasantly. "You're harder to neutralize than projected."

Michael stared at him. "So this was always you."

Kincaid smiled faintly. "No. This was always inevitable."

Michael's gaze flicked past him.

Two suitcases stood in the hallway.

Packed.

Ready.

Naomi followed his eyes—too late.

"You're leaving," Michael said.

Kincaid inclined his head. "Phase One concluded successfully."

Michael's pulse hammered. "The deal."

"Finalized," Kincaid said smoothly. "Signed. Distributed. Buried under layers you'll never reach."

Michael turned back to Naomi. "You knew."

Her voice dropped. "I knew you wouldn't stop if you suspected."

"You tried to kill me."

Kincaid shrugged lightly. "We tried to remove an obstacle."

"And Monica?" Michael demanded. "What threat did she pose?"

"You brought her into this, and she saw too much," Kincaid replied. "That's dangerous."

Michael swallowed hard. "You think you've won."

Kincaid's gaze sharpened—pleased. "Don't be childish, Michael. You're simply too late."

Michael felt the weight of it settle.

No proof.

No office.

No authority.

Trevor compromised.

Evidence erased.

Narrative rewritten.

"You won't be believed," Kincaid continued calmly. "Your investigator has already been flagged. Your credibility is being dissolved as we speak. And by the time anyone realizes what's happening—"

He paused, letting it land.

"Phase Two will already be underway."

Michael's voice was steady. "You're talking about lives."

Kincaid smiled. "History is rarely bloodless."

Naomi's hands trembled at her sides.

"This was never meant to go this far," she said.

Kincaid didn't look at her. "Progress never asks permission."

Michael straightened as much as his body allowed.

"This ends," he said.

Kincaid met his gaze. "Not tonight."

Michael turned toward the door.

Behind him, Kincaid spoke one final time.

"You were right about one thing, Michael. Pressure reveals fault lines."

Michael didn't turn back.

"And arrogance," he said quietly, "reveals judgment."

He stepped into the night.

Now he understood.

Naomi wasn't the architect.

She was the access point.

And the war had already begun.

Michael's phone was in his hand as he moved.

Monica needed him.

Trevor needed warning.

He stepped onto the front walk and checked his screen.

No signal.

He refreshed once. Then again.

Nothing.

Behind him, Kincaid chuckled softly.

"Ah," he said, almost kindly. "That'll be temporary."

Michael turned.

Kincaid was already reaching for his coat. "Naomi," he called back into the house, voice calm, unhurried. "Finish getting dressed. We're on schedule."

The door closed.

It was then that Michael finally understood just how alone they intended him to be.

27

The Long Night

MONICA

Monica woke to silence.

The hollow kind—the kind that rang too loudly in her ears. The microwave clock glowed 3:07 a.m.

Her first thought was of Michael.

She sat up, heart already racing, and listened.

Nothing.

No movement from the guest room. No creak of floorboards. No low murmur of someone shifting in pain, the way Michael always did before settling again.

"Michael?" she whispered.

The name vanished into the dark.

She pushed the blanket aside and stood, every sense sharpening as she crossed the room. The safe house was small but unfamiliar, and unfamiliar spaces had learned how to make her nervous fast.

The guest room was empty.

The bed was untouched.

Cold.

Her pulse spiked. "No... no, no..."

She moved faster now, padding down the hall, checking the bathroom, the kitchen, the back door. Still locked. Still secure. Nothing disturbed.

Except—

A folded piece of paper lay on the counter.

Her name was written across the front in Michael's handwriting.

Her breath caught as she picked it up.

Her hands trembled as she read it.

Trust me.

She grabbed her phone and dialed immediately.

Busy signal.

She tried again.

Busy.

Again.

Nothing.

Fear crept in—wrapping itself around her ribs and tightening with every breath.

"God," she whispered, pressing her forehead to the counter. "Please. Please don't let this be another fire."

She forced herself to breathe. To think.

Michael wouldn't act blindly. He wouldn't leave without reason. And he wouldn't abandon her. Especially after everything they'd already walked through together.

Still, the silence pressed in.

She prayed again, softer this time—all she could ask for was steadiness. The kind of prayer you prayed when faith had to hold without proof.

Nearly an hour passed.

Then, headlights swept across the front window.

Monica was on her feet before the engine cut.

The door opened quietly.

Michael stepped into the kitchen, face drawn, shoulders tight, eyes carrying something she'd never seen before.

Relief hit her so hard it nearly stole her breath.

"Michael."

She crossed the room in three steps and stopped just short of touching him, searching his face. "Where did you go? I couldn't reach you. Your phone—"

"I know," he said quietly. "It was blocked."

Her stomach dropped. "Blocked?"

He nodded once. "I went to Naomi's house."

The words landed like a stone.

"You did what?" she whispered.

"I needed confirmation," he said. "And I got it."

He set his phone on the counter like it was evidence instead of a device. "She wasn't alone."

Monica's chest tightened. "Who?"

"Gavin Kincaid."

Her breath stalled.

"That's not possible," she said automatically. "You said he stepped down from the board years ago."

Michael shook his head. "Apparently, he never left. He was running it from behind the curtain the whole time."

He leaned back against the counter, eyes dark. "They were packing. Suitcases in the hallway. Naomi wasn't being removed—she was being extracted."

Cold seeped into her bones.

"He told me it was already done," Michael continued. "The approvals. The shell transfers. The land. Phase One."

Her voice barely worked. "Phase one of what?"

Michael met her eyes.

"Whatever comes next," he said. "He didn't say, but Kincaid made it very clear it can't be stopped. That no one will believe me. That Trevor's been neutralized. That Jonah's gone."

Monica swallowed hard. "And the fire?"

"They meant to kill us," he said. No anger. No drama. Just truth. "The accident. The fire at your house. This wasn't about pressure. It was meant to be an execution."

The word hung between them.

She stepped closer then—no hesitation now—and placed her hand flat against his chest, grounding them both.

"They were wrong about one thing," she said quietly.

Michael looked at her.

"You're not alone," she continued. "And neither am I. God didn't pull us out of fire just to abandon us in the dark."

Something shifted in his expression.

It wasn't softness that settled there.

It was resolve.

"They're moving faster now," he said. "Which means they'll make mistakes."

"And so will we," Monica replied. "If we rush."

She met his gaze, steady and unafraid.

"So we don't," she said. "We pray. We wait. And when Trevor gets back, we listen to what he's found before we make a move."

Michael nodded once.

"Because if Kincaid was that calm," he said quietly, "it means something's already in motion. Trevor will see what I can't."

Michael exhaled slowly, the weight of the night settling into something heavier—but clearer.

Outside, the world was still dark.

But dawn was coming.

And whatever it brought, they would meet it together.

28

Inheritance

NAOMI

The house no longer felt like hers.

Naomi stood in the upstairs bedroom, hands braced on the edge of the dresser, listening to the quiet settle after Michael Lawson's departure. It wasn't peaceful silence—it was the hollow kind, the air that followed destruction, when everything looked intact, but nothing was.

Michael's words still echoed.

They tried to kill me.

You knew.

She closed her eyes.

Downstairs, drawers opened and shut with methodical precision. Her father moved through the house like a man untouched by confrontation, by accusation, by proximity to consequence.

Gavin Kincaid had not raised his voice when Michael stood in their living room.

He hadn't needed to.

Naomi straightened and crossed to the closet. Half of it was already empty. Two suitcases lay open on the bed, clothing folded with a care that felt grotesque given the urgency humming beneath everything.

"You should've finished packing before he arrived," Gavin said from the doorway.

She turned.

He leaned against the frame, jacket already on, phone in hand. Calm. Immaculate. Untethered.

"He shouldn't have been here," she said.

"And yet he was," Gavin replied mildly. "That's the problem with men like Michael Lawson. They don't know when to stop believing the world owes them fairness."

Naomi's throat tightened. "You told me this was contained."

"It is," he said. "Just not in the way you hoped."

She zipped the first suitcase harder than necessary. "You said there would be no collateral."

Gavin's gaze sharpened—the warmth draining from it.

"Naomi. You're still thinking in terms of proximity."

She turned to face him fully. "My house. Michael's life. Monica Greene's home burned to the ground. You call that *proximity*?"

Gavin stepped into the room, lowering his voice. "That woman is a variable. Michael made her one."

"And Jonah?" Naomi asked. "He's gone. He copied files."

"Yes," Gavin said. "And he'll run until running no longer works."

Something cold settled in Naomi's chest.

"This wasn't supposed to get personal," she said.

Gavin smiled faintly. "It was always personal. You just didn't know who it was personal for."

She shook her head. "Michael trusted us."

"He trusted systems," Gavin corrected. "And systems exist to be leveraged."

The truth pressed in, heavy and unavoidable.

This wasn't about a deal.

It had never been.

"The attack," Naomi said slowly. "What you're planning—it's already in motion."

"Yes."

Her pulse spiked. "You said Phase Two wouldn't move until the board was aligned."

Gavin's phone buzzed. He glanced at it, then slipped it back into his pocket.

"The board is irrelevant now," he said. "The acquisitions served their purpose. Signatures were convenient, not essential."

Naomi stared at him. "Michael will talk."

"Michael will shout into a system that no longer listens," Gavin replied. "The DOJ agent is now compromised. Jonah is missing. And by morning, Michael Lawson will officially be a displaced executive grieving the loss of his woman's home."

Naomi's breath hitched."They tried to kill him."

"Yes," Gavin said calmly. "And failed."

Her voice dropped. "You won't try again?"

Gavin studied her long enough for the answer to settle before he spoke.

"Naomi," he said evenly, "this ends one of two ways. Either Michael steps out of the picture... or the picture becomes too large for him to matter."

She backed away a step. "People will notice."

"They always do," he said. "Afterward."

Her hands trembled. She curled them into fists. "This is bigger than Vanguard."

Gavin nodded. "It always was."

She thought of Michael standing in her living room—bloodied once, unbowed twice. Of the way he'd looked at her, not with hatred, but with disbelief and betrayal.

I was good to you.

"You used me," she said quietly.

Gavin tilted his head. "I prepared you."

"For this?" she asked. "For murder?"

"For inheritance," he replied.

The word landed like a sentence.

"We leave now," Gavin continued. "The city will become inconvenient soon."

Naomi looked around the room one last time. At the life she had curated. At the illusion of control she had mistaken for power.

"What if he's right?" she asked. "What if this doesn't stay contained?"

Gavin picked up one of the suitcases. "Then history will blame infrastructure. Or incompetence. Or God."

He paused at the door.

"If you want protection in what comes next," he said without turning, "you'll stand where you belong."

He left.

Naomi zipped the second suitcase with shaking hands.

Somewhere beyond the walls of the house, systems were already shifting.

Lights would flicker. Signals would fail. People would ask questions too late.

And for the first time since stepping into her role at Vanguard, Naomi understood the truth she could no longer escape.

She hadn't just enabled something dangerous. She had helped unleash something unstoppable.

29

Burn Lines

MICHAEL

Trevor arrived just after sunrise.

The dogs' sharp, sudden barking cut through the quiet, all instinct and urgency.

Michael didn't turn right away. He already knew.

No knock. No warning. Just the soft scrape of a key in the lock and the door opening with practiced efficiency.

He didn't rise from the chair where he'd spent the last hour staring out the narrow kitchen window, watching a sky that refused to give anything away. Monica stood when Trevor entered, relief flickering across her face—then fading just as quickly when she saw his expression.

Trevor looked like a man who hadn't slept.

His jacket was rumpled. His eyes were sharp in a way that had nothing to do with caffeine. He closed the door behind him and slid the deadbolt into place before he spoke.

"They burned me," he said.

No preamble. No softening.

Monica's hand went to her mouth. Michael felt something settle cold and heavy in his chest.

Monica swallowed. "I can't believe they framed you."

"They did more than that," Trevor said. "They positioned me."

Michael straightened slightly. "For what?"

"For when this breaks," Trevor replied. "Someone needs to be the bad actor inside the DOJ."

The room went quiet.

Michael thought of Naomi's smile. Kincaid's calm certainty.

"I went to see Naomi."

Trevor's head snapped toward him. "Tell me."

Michael crossed the room slowly, measured.

"She wasn't alone," he said. "Gavin Kincaid was there."

Trevor went still.

"The ex-chairman of the board?" he asked.

"One and the same," Michael replied. "Suitcases in the hall. Extraction in progress."

Trevor exhaled through his nose.

"What did he say?"

Michael met his eyes.

"He said Phase One concluded successfully."

Silence fell.

Trevor's jaw flexed once. "Then it's worse than I thought."

Monica's pulse quickened. "What does that mean?"

"It means," Trevor said, "they've already secured their position."

Michael nodded slowly. "The land."

"Yes."

Trevor dropped his bag on the table and unzipped it.

"They wiped my logs overnight," he continued. "Access records altered. Communications rerouted. There was a report filed claiming I mishandled evidence and compromised an active inquiry."

Trevor pulled a folded satellite printout from his bag and spread it across the dining table.

Red markers dotted multiple states.

Monica stepped closer.

"These are the parcels," Trevor said. "Redfield Holdings. Blackridge. Three other shells. All option holders."

Michael leaned in.

"They never owned the land," he said quietly.

"No," Trevor replied. "They owned the option."

Monica swallowed. "The access."

Trevor nodded.

He tapped one marker.

"Substation."

Another.

"Fiber trunk."

Another.

"Regional data relay."

Michael felt it align.

"You're saying they're inside the grid."

Trevor held his gaze.

"I'm saying they're close enough to influence it."

That landed heavier than confirmation.

"If they wanted collapse, they wouldn't bother with proximity," Trevor continued. "There are faster ways to cause chaos."

Michael studied him. "Then what?"

Trevor exhaled slowly.

"My working theory?" he said. "They're aiming for disruption, rather than destruction."

A beat.

"Controlled instability. Enough to shake confidence. Enough to justify intervention."

Monica's voice lowered. "Fracture it."

Trevor nodded once.

"If I'm right, they won't bring the grid down. But they'll make it look unreliable."

Michael's jaw tightened.

"Localized disruptions," Trevor continued. "Signal interference. Data latency. Transaction delays. Rolling instability across multiple regions."

"Which looks like failure," Michael said.

"Yes."

"Systemic failure."

"Yes."

Monica's voice thinned. "Markets."

"Emergency response."

"Transportation."

Trevor gave a tight nod.

"And if it happens in enough places at once..."

Michael finished it.

"Confidence collapses."

Trevor's expression hardened.

"And whoever steps in to stabilize it controls what comes next."

The room felt smaller.

This went far beyond sabotage.

It was succession.

Michael straightened slowly.

"They needed me gone before activation."

"Yes," Trevor replied.

"And they needed *you* compromised before exposure."

"Yes."

Monica's breath came shallow. "So Phase Two..."

Trevor hesitated.

"I don't know the trigger," he admitted. "I don't know the mechanism. But the positioning is complete."

Michael's mind raced.

"The land option expires in less than thirty days."

Trevor looked at him sharply.

"Forty-five with the vote delay," Michael continued. "Which means timing matters."

Monica whispered, "It's a doorway."

"Yes," Trevor said. "And Phase One was securing the doorway."

Michael looked at the red circles again.

Trevor gathered the papers.

"You have to leave," he said.

Michael looked up, surprised.

"You have to leave," Trevor repeated. "Both of you."

Monica stiffened. "And you?"

"I stay visible," Trevor replied. "If I disappear, I confirm their narrative. If I stay, they assume I'm contained."

Michael's voice lowered. "As what?"

Trevor met his eyes.

"Bait."

"No," Monica said immediately.

"It's the only play left," Trevor replied. "They think I'm scrambling. Let them."

Michael stood, ignoring the flare of pain in his leg. As much as he hated to admit it, he knew Trevor was right.

"I have property in Colorado," he said. "Off-grid. Remote."

Trevor nodded once. "Good."

Monica looked at Michael, realization dawning. "The maps in your bedside table."

"Yes."

Trevor zipped his bag closed.

"Go before the next phase becomes visible," he said. "Because once it does, you won't be able to move freely."

Michael extended his hand. Trevor clasped it firmly.

"Whatever they're planning," Trevor said quietly, "it won't look intentional."

Michael's gaze hardened.

"Then we'll recognize it before anyone else does."

Trevor gave a single nod and slipped out.

The door closed behind him.

Monica turned to Michael, fear and resolve braided tight.

"Colorado," she said.

"Yes."

Outside, the sun crested the horizon—bright, indifferent.

Across the country, substations hummed.

Fiber lines carried silent traffic.

Markets prepared to open.

Everything looked stable.

Phase Two was on its own timetable.

And somewhere, someone was already watching the clock.

30

The Line Held

MICHAEL

They didn't stop driving until the sky went gray.

Colorado unfolded as a series of dark roads and quiet fuel stations—no names, no conversations, just motion. Michael let Trevor's voice replay in his head as the miles stacked up in the passenger seat.

You don't disappear. You stay visible. Let them think you're contained.

Michael understood now what that really meant.

By dusk, they pulled into a small, nondescript lodge tucked against a stand of pines—temporary housing Michael had used once, years ago, for a deal that never materialized. It wasn't on any map that mattered. No reservations system. No front desk questions.

Just shelter.

The dogs leapt out of the car, shaking off the stiffness of hours confined to the back seat, noses already working as they fanned out across the unfamiliar space.

Inside, the air smelled faintly of cedar and old coffee. Monica locked the door behind them and leaned her weight into it for a moment, as if making sure the world stayed outside.

Michael lowered himself into a chair slowly, his leg screaming in protest. He welcomed the pain. Pain kept him present. Pain kept him honest.

Monica set their bags down without speaking. She moved through the room with purpose—checking windows, drawing curtains, setting their phones face-down on the counter. When she finished, she turned to him.

"I called Trevor," she said. "Straight to voicemail."

Michael nodded. "Hopefully, that means he's still upright."

She studied him. "And you?"

He didn't answer right away.

The silence shrouded them like a heavy blanket—comfortable yet full. He understood then that remaining visible wouldn't stop what was coming—it would only decide who else got hurt.

"I can't stay in this," he said finally. "Not the way I am."

Monica didn't interrupt.

"They're already rewriting the narrative," he continued. "By noon, they probably labeled me as a displaced executive. By tomorrow, unstable. By next week, a liability with a tragic story and no credibility."

She crossed the room and sat across from him. "You've known that since Naomi's house."

"Yes," he said. "But knowing it isn't the same as accepting what it costs."

He leaned forward, forearms braced on his knees.

"I've spent my life believing the right thing to do was to stay in the room. To confront. To argue. To put my name on the line and trust that truth would carry it."

Monica's voice was quiet. "And now?"

"And now," he said, "my presence makes this easier for them. I give them a face to smear. A story to control. A villain to point at while they move."

She let that settle.

"So what are you saying?" she asked.

Michael exhaled slowly. "I'm saying I have to step away before they push me out. Quietly. On my terms."

Monica nodded once in understanding.

She never wondered what would happen next. The only question was whether she was willing to be present when it did.

She was.

Michael pulled his phone from his pocket and unlocked it, fingers steady. A resignation letter—already drafted, already revised a dozen times during the long ride—waited on the screen.

"I'll submit it at first light," he said. "No press. No statement. I relinquish authority, sever my remaining board ties, and disappear before they can turn it into a spectacle."

Monica felt the weight of it then—the price hidden beneath the strategy.

"You built that company," she said softly.

"I stewarded it," he corrected. "That season is over."

For a moment, something tightened behind his ribs—the recognition of what it meant to lay it down. Years of early mornings, difficult calls, decisions made for people he would never meet, all set down at once. He didn't mourn the loss of power. He mourned the leaving of a post he had guarded faithfully.

He hesitated, then added, "There are certain assets I can't move without triggering alerts. I'll just leave them. Let them think they won."

Her jaw tightened. "And your name?"

He met her gaze. "They'll drag it through the mud."

She didn't look away. "Are you ready for that?"

Michael closed his eyes briefly.

Lord, he prayed without words, if this is obedience, give me the strength not to fight it.

When he opened them again, the answer was already there—steady, unshakable resolve.

"Yes," he said.

They sat in that truth together as night settled fully around the lodge, the wind moving through the trees outside in long, unhurried breaths.

Exhaustion claimed them in stages—Monica taking the bed, Michael settling carefully onto the couch, pain and fatigue finally pulling him under. The lodge held its silence through the night, steady and unintrusive.

Morning came quietly.

Thin light filtered through the curtains, pale and cold against the mountains.

Michael woke gently, the decision still heavy—but no longer crushing. From where he lay, he could see the edge of the doorway, the soft glow spilling in from the bathroom.

He listened to the sound of running water, the ordinary rhythm of it, and felt something loosen in his chest. What rose in its place was gratitude—for her steadiness, her presence, and the quiet choice she had made to stay when leaving would have been easier.

Monica emerged a few minutes later, already dressed, already composed. She met his eyes and gave him a warm smile, as if acknowledging the night they'd survived.

She reached for her phone. "Trevor will need time. He'll surface when he can."

"And when he does," Michael said, pushing himself carefully to his feet, "we won't be anywhere near the blast radius."

She took a breath. "Good."

Michael picked up his phone, opened the draft, and read it one last time. Then he sent the email.

No ceremony. No confirmation ping. Just a clean release into the system that had once been his.

The moment passed.

Nothing exploded.

The world didn't end.

And yet—everything shifted.

They packed again—lighter this time. Fewer assumptions. Fewer attachments.

As they stepped back outside, the sun finally broke through the cloud cover, pale and cold against the mountains.

Michael paused at the edge of the porch, taking it in the stillness. The space between noise and purpose.

He understood it now.

This was a repositioning.

Behind them, systems were already shifting. Stories were already being written. Lines were being crossed.

But ahead of them was something different.

A narrow road.

A quieter place.

And the kind of obedience that didn't announce itself—but held fast when everything else burned.

Michael reached for Monica's hand.

She took it without hesitation.

They drove north.

EPILOGUE

When the Lights Begin to Dim

The first outage wasn't dramatic.

No explosions. No sirens. No headlines crawling across glowing screens.

Just a flicker.

In a quiet suburb outside Raleigh, a streetlight blinked once—twice—then went dark. A man paused mid-step on his evening walk, frowned at the sky, and kept moving.

In Oregon, a data center logged a minor anomaly. A technician flagged it, tagged it low priority, and went home on time.

In New Jersey, a commuter train stalled for ninety seconds before lurching forward again. Someone muttered about infrastructure. Someone else joked about systems that never worked the way they were promised.

Across the country, systems corrected themselves.

For now.

* * *

The sky was just beginning to pale when they reached Fairplay.

Monica guided the SUV along the narrowing road, hands steady on the wheel as pavement gave way to gravel, then to something older—less interested in convenience, more concerned with endurance. Pines pressed in on both sides, the land rising quietly around them.

Michael watched the road ahead, familiarity settling in his chest long before the house came into view.

"There," he said, nodding toward a break in the tree line.

Monica slowed.

The gate was unmarked—steel set back far enough to miss if you didn't know it was there. There were no signs, no lights—only the quiet assertion of steel.

Michael reached into the center console and pulled out a small remote, worn at the edges. He handed it to her.

"Hold it down until it opens," he said.

She did.

The gate slid back without a sound.

Monica glanced at him.

They passed through, the gate closing behind them with a soft finality that felt less like confinement and more like protection. The road climbed gently now, winding upward through open acreage.

As they crested the rise, the house revealed itself—wood and stone, broad and grounded, sitting above the land as if it had always belonged there. A wraparound deck caught the early light, the valley beyond it stretching wide beneath a sky still deciding what it would become.

The sun edged higher, brushing the snow-dusted peaks with gold.

Monica slowed to a stop without being told.

She stepped out first, turning slowly, taking in the land—the distance, the fencing, the quiet. Moose tracks cut through the frost near the tree line. The air was sharp, clean, demanding attention.

"It feels... set apart," she said quietly.

Michael joined her.

"I bought it years ago," he said. "Quietly. After my first board term. No holding company. No development plans."

She looked at him.

"I didn't know what I'd need it for," he continued. "Only that someday, I might need a place that didn't answer to anyone else's system."

A pause.

"I hoped I'd never have to use it."

"This isn't a hideout," Monica said.

"No," Michael agreed. "It's a refuge."

By the time they stood on the back porch, the sun had fully cleared the ridge. Light spilled across the mountains—steady, unhurried—touching peaks that had outlasted every empire built below them.

The thin mountain air burned clean in Michael's lungs.

Monica joined him without a word, her presence steady as the ground beneath their feet. She pulled her jacket tighter around her.

They stood side by side, watching the morning take shape as the dogs moved easily through the open land below the porch, unconfined and unafraid. It was as if the space itself had been waiting for them.

"Trevor left a message," she said quietly.

Michael nodded. "I hoped he would call."

"Three substations," she continued. "Synchronized irregularities. Nothing official yet."

"Nothing ever is," he said. "Until it's too late to pretend otherwise."

She studied his profile. "Are you afraid?"

Michael considered her question for a long moment.

He thought of Naomi's house. Of Gavin Kincaid's calm certainty. Of the moment his phone had gone dead in his hand—the silence swallowing the last thread of control he'd thought he had.

"Yes," he said at last. "But not the way I was."

She waited.

"I'm afraid of what this will cost," he continued. "Not just us. Everyone who won't get a warning."

Monica stepped closer, their shoulders touching. No hesitation. No retreat.

"I'm not afraid of standing," she said.

He turned to her then. Really turned. The woman who had pulled him from twisted metal. Who had lost her home without losing herself. Who had stepped into the fire with eyes open and faith intact.

"You were right," he said quietly. "God didn't spare me just to keep me breathing."

She gave a small, knowing smile. "He rarely does."

Michael reached for her hand.

Whatever came next—whatever broke, whatever burned, whatever failed—this was not a moment for half-steps or hedging.

"I don't know what kind of world we're waking up into," he said. "But I know this—if I'm walking through it, I want you beside me. Everything feels easier with you by my side, and there's no one I'd rather weather this storm with."

Monica's fingers laced through his, gentle but certain. She leaned into him, resting there as if the ground beneath them had already proven trustworthy.

"I was sent," she said quietly. "And I'm still here."

He wrapped an arm around her shoulders, something steadying deep in his chest.

"We don't run," she continued. "We don't fracture. We stay. We listen. And we move when we're called."

A pause. A breath.

"We weather it—together."

The vow settled between them, quiet and sure.

Unshaken. Enduring.

The kind of promise that holds when everything else gives way.

Behind them, inside the house, the radio crackled once.

Then again.

Static surged—sharp, sudden.

A voice broke through, partial and strained.

"...regional outage...unconfirmed...advising—"

Static swallowed the rest.

Silence rushed in to take its place.

Monica closed her eyes.

Michael bowed his head.

"Lord," he prayed, voice steady against the wind, "we don't know the shape of what's coming. But You do. Make us faithful with what we've been given. Brave enough to act. Humble enough to listen."

Monica whispered, "And strong enough to endure."

The wind moved through the pines.

The world kept turning.

But something had begun.

And grace—quiet, relentless, unyielding—was already moving to meet it.

Sneak Peek: Grounded by Grace [Book 2]

Prologue

One Week Earlier

The house sat alone on a mountainside, hidden deep within the Wyoming wilderness.

From a distance, it appeared to be nothing more than another luxury mountain retreat—glass, steel, and timber rising from the pines.

Appearances rarely told the whole story.

The property operated independently from the electrical grid. Its water came from a private well drilled hundreds of feet beneath the mountain. Satellite communications replaced traditional networks. Layers of security remained invisible unless someone knew where to look.

Every detail had been designed for privacy.

Every system had been built for continuity.

Gavin Kincaid stood beside a wall of glass overlooking a valley painted silver by moonlight. The view stretched for miles across untouched wilderness, beautiful enough to distract most people.

Kincaid had never been most people.

Behind him, a sleek marble fireplace cast a warm glow across the open living space. Maps, intelligence reports, and handwritten notes covered the dining table.

Across the room, Naomi slept peacefully on a sectional positioned near the fire.

For the first time in weeks, she looked rested.

Kincaid envied her ability to sleep.

The satellite phone vibrated once against the table.

He picked it up immediately.

"Report."

The voice on the other end was calm.

Measured.

Professional.

One of the reasons Kincaid valued him.

"Lawson remains off-grid."

Kincaid's eyes drifted to the map spread before him.

Colorado.

Several locations had been circled. Several more had been crossed out.

Michael Lawson had vanished somewhere among those mountains.

Resourceful men survived longer than expected.

Resourceful men created complications.

"Any movement?"

"No."

The Observer paused.

"We lost his trail eleven days ago."

Kincaid's mouth tightened.

Long enough to become frustrating.

Short enough to remain dangerous.

"And Hale?"

The answer came immediately.

"Still active."

There it was.

The problem.

Lawson had chosen isolation.

Trevor Hale was still moving.

Still searching.

Still assembling pieces that were never meant to fit together.

Kincaid rested both hands on the table.

"How much does he know?"

"Enough."

The word settled heavily between them.

Enough.

A handful of facts in the right order could dismantle years of preparation.

Kincaid glanced toward Naomi.

She shifted slightly in her sleep before settling again.

Good.

His attention returned to the map.

"We're approaching the final window."

The Observer remained silent.

He understood exactly what that meant.

"Hale cannot interfere."

"He won't."

Kincaid's gaze hardened.

"I need more than confidence."

A brief pause followed.

Then:

"Give me a timeline."

"Forty-eight hours."

The house fell silent.

The fire crackled softly inside the stone hearth.

Forty-eight hours.

Years of planning would finally be set in motion in just two days.

Two days until execution.

Two days until every moving piece reached its assigned position.

Two days until momentum became irreversible.

The Observer spoke first.

"I'll find him."

Kincaid studied the map.

Somewhere beyond those mountains, Michael Lawson remained alive.

Somewhere between here and there, Trevor Hale was moving.

Eventually, their paths would intersect.

Men carried their priorities with them.

Sooner or later, those priorities revealed the destination.

"If Hale reconnects with Lawson," Kincaid said, "containment becomes significantly more difficult."

"It won't happen."

"It *can't* happen."

The distinction mattered.

The Observer understood.

"I'll contain it."

Kincaid finally looked away from the map.

The darkened glass reflected the room behind him—the firelight, the scattered papers, the sleeping woman across the room.

A lifetime of decisions had led here.

A lifetime of sacrifices.

A lifetime of patience.

"Good," he said quietly.

"Because in forty-eight hours, none of this can be stopped."

The line disconnected.

Kincaid lowered the phone and stood motionless for a long moment.

Outside, wind moved through the trees.

The mountains remained silent.

Patient.

His gaze settled once more on Colorado.

On Michael Lawson.

On Trevor Hale.

The pieces were moving.

And somewhere beyond those mountains, a man who knew too much was still free.

About the Author

Chanel Jones is a writer, storyteller, and creative entrepreneur with a passion for stories that explore faith, resilience, and the quiet courage it takes to stand for truth when the cost is high. *Collision of Grace* is her debut Christian thriller, blending suspense, emotional depth, and themes of grace under pressure into a story that asks what happens when ordinary lives collide with extraordinary danger.

In addition to writing fiction, Chanel is the founder of Jones & Jones Publishing and the creator of the *Pico & Friends* children's book series, known for its heartfelt stories centered on belonging, courage, and emotional growth.

When she's not writing, Chanel enjoys strong coffee, sunny weather, meaningful conversations, and creating stories that leave readers thinking long after the final page.

You can connect with me on:

https://chaneljoneswrites.com

https://www.facebook.com/chaneljoneswrites

www.ingramcontent.com/pod-product-compliance
Lightning Source LLC
LaVergne TN
LVHW031343150826
845673LV00009B/2846

* 9 7 9 8 9 9 4 7 4 9 6 8 5 *